For my Boyfriend
Brad. Eng iy;

Fated
Connections
Installment 1
By Janette Harjo

Dedication

The names are too many to list, but I would like to dedicate this, my first published work, to all those who have helped me with this as teachers, readers, critiquers, and motivators. Especially to my sister Judy Crowe who beta read for me, my mother Annie Mae Simon who inspired me in my writing, and to Romance Writers of America for enabling me to have met all those who have assisted in my journey to publication.

Prologue

1690's American colonies-
Alecksander Stone, the new world's foremost witch-hunter, sat on his steed atop a rugged slope. The spirited animal tossed its head and pranced in place.

The dark-haired man held his horse at point. It alerted its attention as he looked down upon the small township of Smithton, Massachusetts.

Time spent with shamans worldwide gave Alecksander a supernatural ability to pinpoint practitioners of witchcraft. He mystified and commanded attention from all who came into contact with him.

Awed by his capabilities, no one questioned the man's unusual talents. Instead, they thanked the tall, fit stranger for coming

1

to their aid as he rid them of the
devil's acolytes.

Chapter One

Same day, outside the village of Smithton, Massachusetts –
Valerie Baldwin tilted her linen-capped head to the mistress of the cottage. The humble two-room timber abode lay on the outskirts of the Smithton, Massachusetts Township.

"Fare thee well, ma-am. I believe thy daughter be without trouble in her head until my next visit to counsel with her.

"Be sure to send for me if she returns to her ways or ye have need for more of my comfort and attention to her."

Valerie took the poor woman's weathered hand between her two soft palms. "Ye can believe in my word, she be not witched, like I hear talk of amongst the Smithton colonists."

3

Though she fought it, the "talk" Valerie overheard set her nerves on edge. But she kept herself strong for her clients' sake. *I must not show my apprehension to Sarah, lest it upset her.*

To this day, Valerie saw success as she held fear of the stories at bay. Although, it seemed to the young brunette as if rumors crouched at her door in wait to devour her.

I ken this talk of such blockish foolery be about me.

"There be no such thing as witches," she informed the matron in a quick breath.

Sarah, the simple woman she spoke to, quickly nodded and glanced toward her front door in an obvious effort to speed her visitor on her way.

Valerie noted the woman's surreptitious gaze. She cringed when the woman put more guilt on her with that same look when she looked into her face.

In spite of her distinct cognizance, Valerie made it a point to not give away she noticed. "Fare thee well."

Valerie lifted her coarse wool blend skirt out of her way

with a quick swoosh. She turned
her back on Sarah and descended
the porch steps with her head held
high.

She spoke aloud to herself as
she made her way from the cottage.
"Mayhap it should concern me, but
I won't pay heed to such untrue
stories." She clenched her fists.
I be not convicted by my gifts.

Even for all her best
portrayal of no worries, Valerie's
gut clenched into an insufferable
knot. In an effort to set herself
at ease, she turned her thoughts
to the children she loved.

*How might I help them through
their current dilemma?* Her
attention first settled on Sarah's
troubled daughter. The girl's
afflictions puzzled the young
healer.

*'Tis as if she has no control
over her actions.* The misery the
girl suffered included involuntary
body tics and instances when she
blurted out unexpected
obscenities.

Valerie turned to face the
home she vacated. She startled
when she noticed Sarah followed
her out onto her porch. The
matron swooshed her arms, as if

she desired to sweep Valerie away without further delay.

The young healer remembered her good manners, smiled and waved to the woman who wrung her hands together. Valerie winced at the matron's illustrated impatience with her departure. Her heart-rate increased.

The middle-aged woman of the house spewed forth quick words, "Good Day to ye, Miss Valerie." She gave a quick wave, then spun her compact body around and hurried back into her home. Valerie jerked at the hasty way Sarah slammed her door between them.

She froze in shock and considered the sense of urgency in Sarah's voice. She also recalled the woman's actions, and realized she should have seen and expected Sarah's abrupt end to their conversation.

Valerie shrugged and remembered her other duties of the day. Then she hurried on her way to the next troubled changeling.

It seems an epidemic of sorts amongst the young ones these days. "I have no more time for my worry with Sarah today," she mumbled to herself.

"Could it be dreams of hard times on their ships be the cause the young ones wake up changed?" Valerie used her speculation as a place to start.

She set her good judgment to work on a reason she could concentrate on. *If verily 'tis in their minds, I must reach and help them before the noose befalls them.*

Valerie became thoughtful as she travelled through the unconquered land. She gazed on the terrain with gratitude.

I be so glad we left the old world for this one. It promises so much beyond freedom of religion and from oppressive government.

She knew the exhilarating landscape of such an unchanged country should have left her without breath. But the distrust she witnessed on Sarah's face troubled her. It brought with it recollections of the talk Valerie knew existed in Smithton.

I wonder wherefore any of the colonists would suspect me of witchcraft? She debated the viewpoint with herself and weighed the social aspects of her way of life as a single, unmarried woman.

Chapter Two

Valerie bemoaned her particular set of circumstances. Her inability to bear a child, and her shame as an unfit wife because of that, plagued her. *Verily the colonists must know the solitary way I live cannot be helped!*

Her current state of affairs, because of life with and without her previous husband, tied her stomach into knots. Its weight sickened her.

No man will have me. The colonists only seek my company when they require my unique talent.

Her ability to be self-sufficient gave her a source of pride she relied on. Valerie rose with the sun on every morning, tended her garden and worked on her home.

She finished her work about her cottage and put her tools away each day by noon. In the afternoons she saw to the afflicted children.

She visualized herself as she talked to the parents of the tormented children. They didn't understand their children's plights, but *she* did.

Valerie's empathic soul heard their pleas, "Pray thee; help our child! We don't ken her." She knew they were poor folk and couldn't offer much for her services. Their swallowed pride humbled her as they begged on their loved one's behalf.

On such occasions, Valerie enfolded each worried woman's hands between her two palms. While the husband looked on, she answered, "What ye give will suffice."

Their delighted response always came back to her the same, "Praise be! But how can ye offer such charity?"

"I offer my services because of my love for children. I can bear none of my own, and accept 'tis my duty in this life to assist distressed children through their hard times.

"'Tis a shared relationship in which we all benefit. As I cherish and console them, they do the same for me."

"But we must give ye something. Surely ye need a little to stay clothed and fed? Be there nothing we can offer in exchange for ye service to us?"

Valerie smiled with her next words, "I live a simple life without much need. I have a home and garden I tend to."

She recalled how he'd then brush her common clothes with a hand, and tell them, "'Tis inexpensive and does me well.

"I'm an itinerant woman of medical counsel by choice. I knew this would be a job of little pay when I chose it. What ye are able to give will suffice.

"I can't bear to think of it, if my existence and assistance to the children I love became too much of a burden to ye."

In the midst of her memories, Valerie's simple skirt caught on a fallen branch and jerked her feet from beneath her.

She regained her sense of balance with outstretched arms. Her near accident brought her awareness of the present back to her mind.

Whether she wanted to give it credence or not, the probability the settlers suspected her of witchery frightened her. *I cannot ken wherefore they should think so.*

Then she enlightened. *Of course. How could I be so blockish? 'Tis because of my ability to attain a healing connection with the children through their thoughts.* She slapped a hand to her forehead.

"Wherefore can I not see so far sometimes?" Her troubled foresight returned from before she perceived suspicion in the previous cottage. She massaged her moist forehead.

"Wherefore 'tis I be the only one these abilities visit themselves on?" But for all her anxiety, Valerie's priorities always concerned the children, to whom her worries returned.

She mulled their conditions over in vision of the way of their unexpected outbursts and fits. *They tear at their skin and make grotesque faces as if they mean threat to those near them.*

Her heart paced with the demonic urgency in each child's plight. She fought not to allow panic to take possession, but fretful knowledge of her own like-predicament remained ever-present in her mind.

The fear of witchcraft hath reached frenzied proportions in the village. But Valerie persevered in spite of her knowledge and continued in her ways.

Valerie's innate sensitivities sent her constant reminders of her self-claimed duties because of "her ways." The children needed her skills, so they wouldn't end up in a place like Bedlam.

Up until recently, she believed the parents knew she loved their children. By way of that love, she worked with them to save their sanity.

In the midst of her considerations, Valerie climbed atop a small wooded knoll. Below her, she saw a group of young people from Smithton. They stood gathered together.

"Look!" one of the older boys shouted. "Up there! In those trees!"

Valerie looked up into a group of trees. It stood behind and to the side of her grove. But she saw nothing unusual.

The rest of the young people soon joined in with the first. *They cluster around the bigger boy with amazed shouts. I wonder 'tis they imagine.*

"It's a flying broomstick! There it goes!" they all clamoured in unison. "It must belong to a witch!"

The first turned to the rest. With an upheld hand, he quieted them.

Chapter Three

Try as she might; Valerie couldn't clearly hear what the young man at the forefront of the group said to the younger ones who sat at his feet.

They came to a sudden silence. She tensed when those assembled turned, and stared in her direction with dropped jaws and pointed fingers. They screamed and raced off into a group of trees far from Valerie.

She placed the back of one hand to her forehead. Her head lightened. Her heart fluttered. She willed a faint to not be so and looked to find what they indicated.

There be no one up here but me. She laid a hand over her chest in awareness of its start. *Could they mean me?*

How could they see her? She
cast a panicked gaze around and
imagined her invisibility in the
grove of trees.
*Verily, it must be their
imaginations run wild in their
free time.* Many more things flew
through Valerie's mind as she
watched.
*Wherefore be they not home
tending their chores?* Regardless
of her curiosity about their
expected daily duties, the young
healer's heart went out to those
children. *'Tis bad their lives be
not more ordered.*
She reasoned, "They should
not have such time to indulge in
fantasy that runs with them. I
fear they soon become afflicted
like the others."
Valerie continued with her
spoken thoughts, as she had become
wont to do for company in the
years of her forced solitude.
"The township children be
unfortunate for their
imaginations. I do wish they
still visited with me. I could
help them. I could calm their
hearts."
Her words went on as she
began her trip home, "They
wouldn't be susceptible to let

their idle minds run with troublesome fantasies."

Valerie's worries continued on her trip home.   Her trek took her across the small hill and homeward in the opposite direction as the children took.

The healer considered the lone doctor who traveled between the settlements during her otherwise uneventful trip back to her home.   She knew if it weren't for her, the children she just saw and the others too, would go uncared for.

She reasoned it all went for the best.   "The physician who travels from place to place doesn't have the necessary knowledge to toil with those who are afflicted with problems in their minds."

In the few outlying settlements she served; the episodes of deep sadness or lack of connection with others tormented the unfortunates.

It remained an affliction no one understood, herself included. Their townsfolk deemed the unfortunates as Tom's o' Bedlam. She shivered with the thought of those housed in Bethlehem Hospital, in London.

She didn't consider those
afflicted in the colony insane.
But she knew they might be sent to
a place like the old world
hospital for their erratic
behaviour.

"They need only be
understood." She thought the idea
of sending the young ones to a
place like Bedlam, the name most
knew the London hospital by, as
horrid.

"Wherefore be only the
children affected by this
madness?" The mysterious fact
both saddened and delighted
Valerie.

Her work with the afflicted
children caused her sadness
because of their illness; whereas
her favor to work with them
delighted her for those few
precious moments spent at their
sides.

Valerie loved them all to her
full heart's extent. They filled
her existence with happiness. No
shame existed for her because of
her childlessness when she shared
their innocent company.

"'Tis perfect for me at this
place. 'Tis meant I be here. I
thank ye God, for my strength to
endure," she uttered on her path

homeward. Valerie spoke those
words daily for the fortitude they
empowered her with.
       One day as she worked and
swept, a young man from the local
native tribe wandered by. He
stood off to the side, hidden in
some brush, but Valerie knew his
presence.

Chapter Four

Wherefore doesn't he just come out of hiding and speak to me? Valerie gave no sign she noticed her visitor and continued to get her days wood chopped, but her thoughts didn't leave the gaunt native. *Mayhap he be hungry.*

At length, Valerie couldn't ignore him any longer. She looked up in acknowledgement of his presence. "Holla!" she called out to her lone spectator.

The native remained silent and still. *He could be a man carved from wood.* Valerie considered if she hadn't trained herself to be alert of her surroundings, she probably wouldn't have noticed him.

The native folk were quiet and not easily seen. This one didn't appear aggressive. *I think*

*'twould be best if I offered him a
gift from my garden.*
Mayhap he'll be my friend.
Her lonely heart leapt at the
idea. The Good Lord knew Valerie
Baldwin could use some friends.

Valerie propped her braided
brush broom, which she crafted
herself as one of her first home
projects, against a nearby White
Pine tree. She then went to her
garden and plucked a ripe green
bean off its stalk.

On her next glance over to
her potential new friend, she
noticed her action definitely held
his attention. She offered him a
big smile and held the food up to
him. It dangled from between her
fingers like a carrot on the end
of a stick. "Would ye like some?"

Her visitor stared at her.
His eyes sparkled as if full of
curiosity, but he still didn't
move. His stoic expression never
changed.

He doesn't understand me.
Valerie waved him toward her with
her free hand. She hoped for
communication with him while she
held the bean out to him.

The dark man of medium height
wore long thick unruly black
braids. He ventured toward her on

hesitant bare legs at her
invitation. His bright eyes
darted back and forth in obvious
observation of all that surrounded
him with each slow step he took.
        When he stood within an arm's
length from Valerie, he stopped
and held out a hand in what
appeared tentative acceptance.
She released her grip on the
vegetable when he smiled and took
it from her. His head cocked form
side-to-side as he scrutinized his
prize. He put the green bean up
to his face and sniffed it.
        Valerie imagined her
visitor's curiosity could've
arisen from the fact the natives
didn't have this bean in their
supply. She didn't know if any of
the other settlers traded this
crop with them.
        She remembered how she
acquired the green bean during one
of her clandestine trading
sessions with a ship from France.
        He slid the vegetable back
and forth under his nose and took
short sniffs. Valerie shook her
head to infer there wouldn't be
much smell. He nodded in apparent
understanding and placed it near
his opened mouth.

Valerie continued to smile. She nodded to imply the native should put it into his mouth and taste it.

He poked the plant into his mouth and closed his yellowed teeth over it. Its crisp skin cracked between his well-worn teeth. He smiled at its taste and nodded his appreciation.

At her new friend's apparent enjoyment of her gift, Valerie walked back to her garden to bag up a bunch for him.

Even though she didn't hear him, Valerie could tell he followed her close by the tingle of every sensitive hair on the back of her neck.

The bag she used for his share of her green beans came from a supply of pouches she'd hand knitted from the vines in her garden.

She kept the bags piled by the area's outer edge for her use. Valerie filled and folded the top of the small produce container. She turned and offered it to her new friend.

He nodded many times in implied thanks as he accepted her gift. His braids bounced with each movement. But he didn't stay by her side to give her the company she craved.

Instead, he turned and left her alone again. He disappeared in the same silence with which he'd come. Valerie watched after him for a minute, then shrugged her shoulders and returned to her chores.

The firewood she later stacked gave her the reassurance of a warm fire at night, but it only heated her cottage and stream water to boil vegetables for her meals.

The boil for her produce didn't comfort her because the vegetables did little to satisfy her physical being. Neither did the heat do much to warm her spirit.

"I must find some way to put meat on my table." *I do wish they taught girls to hunt and angle for fish at school. I only ken to cook and take care of my home. That does little to put meat on my table.*

Valerie knew if she were to learn, she'd need to teach herself. 'Twill I use for an implement to angle with?" Ships from England didn't come with the frequency Valerie or any of the other settlers would've liked.

She knew she'd not be able to trade for a pole she could fashion to angle with soon enough to suit her. "I shan't wait. I don't need a readymade pole."

Valerie recalled how the occasional fish swim through the waters of her stream. "Now the time has arrived I should catch one of them to cook for my dinner."

When I find a proper limb to angle with; I'll fashion it into a pole. She embarked on a trek into the grove of small white pines nearby her home. – the same woods her recent visitor came from.

She spied an apt looking limb on a supple young tree. The branch Valerie saw appeared flexible and strong. She rubbed her hands together and with great resolve, grabbed the limb and pulled, but the tree didn't give way.

Determined, Valerie wouldn't be deterred by the limb's noncompliance. She yanked at its joint until her feet slid out from under her on the semi-grassy, bark-lined ground.

Soft blue-green needles
dropped from the trees also
covered the hard ground Valerie
landed on. She stared up at the
defiant tree. The limb taunted
her with its near-perfection.
The tree blurred. She
couldn't tell if her reaction came
from the burn in her palms, the
pain in her hind-side, or her
failure. Her face warmed and she
looked about to see if anyone
witnessed her graceless act. She
saw no one.

Chapter Five

Next Morning–
Valerie woke to a bright new day. She jumped up, put on some light leggings and a loose fitted linen bodice. At her door she pulled on a pair of tall woven angling boots she'd traded for at the last ship's visit.

Her well-fitted boots and attire would do well for her day's duties. First on her list would be to explore the trees adjacent to her cottage in search of another perfect tree.

At her home's entrance, Valerie tripped over her feet and leaned on her shoulder against the door jamb. During the night a large leather-wrapped object appeared on her porch.

Valerie threw her hands up to the sides of her face. "'Tis

this?" She stared at the awkward bag. It didn't move, but looked like it could possibly contain a lifeform.

She swallowed hard before she gave the unexpected bundle a timid tap with one of her feet. It didn't give. Breath she didn't realize she'd held escaped her, and her body melted into a relieved puddle at the package's lack of response.

Encouraged by the bag's lack of free will, Valerie knelt down to touch it. Its cool firmness intrigued her. She then took it on herself to perform another act of bravery as she ran her inquisitive hands over the container's bumpy length and breadth.

Her curiosity grew with each stroke. She eventually found an edge on which she might pull to open it. The object unwrapped in an organized fashion with her first gentle tug. It presented her with longed for treasures.

Fresh fish and other raw meats — enough to last her a few days without spoilage - lay before her. She delighted in the fact they appeared prepared and ready to be cooked.

Valerie decided they could be kept in the small cold food storage pit she'd dug under her home. She raised her palms to her cheeks.

"Glory Be! 'Tis verily a gift from Heaven!" She raised her vision heavenward and whispered, "Thank ye, Lord."

After her moment of reverence, she looked around to see if her gift's earthly bearer could be near. No one could be seen, but the scenery blurred as her eyes watered with gratefulness, which overflowed from her heart.

Valerie bundled up the foodstuffs as fast as a squirrel with nuts. She carried it to her pit, and preserved it in the underground's chill.

Her heart pounded with excitement by the time she made her way back into her cottage with a small portion of her find. She eyed the fresh meat with ravenous appreciation.

"There will be meat in my vegetable stew tonight!"

From that day on, whenever her meat supply ran low, it appeared as if by magic at her door. As time passed, she came to

expect it. Even so, she stayed up
late and woke early in the
mornings when she could.

Her effort to keep watch and
see who her benefactor could be,
paid off. It didn't surprise her
when she saw her native friend
arrive one early day with his arms
full.

Valerie ran outside as he
dropped off his presentation for
her. "So 'tis ye who leaves this
for me!" She wrapped her arms
around him in a big hug.

He froze at her sudden
appearance and action.

"I must repay ye!" she
insisted.

The Wampanoag didn't return
her embrace. Instead he stood
still and looked at her in obvious
curiosity of both her action and
words.

"Oh, dear! I forgot ye don't
understand my words." She pointed
to the meat, and then to her
garden, and then back and forth
between the two of them. "I share
my vegetables, and ye supply me
with meat!"

From that time on, the young
native appeared at Valerie's home
without secrecy. It didn't take

long until he also brought along
more of his tribe.
They visited her every couple
of weeks. Each time they came,
they bore more food and remained
eager to help her with the
building chores on her home.
In return for their gifts of
meat and services; Valerie
contributed a bounteous supply of
her vegetables to her native
friends.
****
Kitchi, the Wampanoag man who
befriended Valerie, appreciated
the way his people contributed to
her. He knew they did so out of
admiration for her resolve to take
care of herself.
The Indians, as they knew the
colonists called them, spoke among
themselves at the tribal village.
"Why has this young woman
been cast out by her people? She
is a good hardy woman. Va-ler-ie
would make a good one of us. We
should welcome her into our
tribe," the youngest among them
told the tribal council.
Kitchi also knew his tribe
admired her ability to grow
different foods. Her people
hadn't taught his to plant the
green stick. *The Great Spirit*

gives her the gift to grow good things.

****

Valerie appreciated her native visitors, but she longed for friendship with the matrons in Smithton. Her days in the township left her with mixed emotions. Whenever she approached the matrons there, she found only disdain.

"What cheer?" Valerie greeted two of the mothers of children she counselled, at the market in Smithton.

Mrs. Smith looked down her nose at Valerie and turned her back. "Barren," she remarked in a snobbish nasal tone.

Mrs. Jones did likewise with her own grand declaration after Mrs. Smith's air of self-importance, "I do wish they would get rid of her. My poor Abigail."

"My Sarah, too," Mrs. Smith replied. She then added in a secretive manner, with one of her hands held up to the side of her mouth, "Have ye heard she even mixes with those non-Christian heathens in the wilderness? Tsk-tsk. 'Tis much to be suspicious about."

The volume of the matron's voice didn't match her reserved manner. The two then flounced too far away for Valerie to overhear any more of their vicious comments.

She watched them go, their gathered skirts held up out of their way. *'Tis like they don't even want to be seen near me.* Valerie watched until they were out of her sight.

"I be not a witch!" she called after them. "I be sorry about thy daughters' afflictions! I cannot help I be unable to bear children! For good measure, she blurted, "The natives be good people!"

Valerie slapped her hands to her cheeks in shock after her most private worry escaped her. *Alas! Wherefore did I need express my sorrow for anything might give thought to witchcraft?*

"Ahh!" the audible gasp sounded from all who overheard her. Valerie's face burned, though it did so more with indignation than with embarrassment.

Wherefore can they not see my unusual talent as a gift from God? Surely my ability to nurture

*children, just as their own mother
would, be a direct gift from God.*
She drew herself up to her
full height of five feet five
inches and raised her nose in
mimic of all the self-righteous
settlers in Smithton. Along with
her proud act she renewed her
long-cherished promise to herself.
*I will make a good life for
myself, regardless of their
superstitious attitudes.* She
raised her face heavenward. *I
praise thee God I can read.
'Twill assist me in times of need
for knowledge and companionship.*
She also took comfort in the
words of the late Queen Mary of
England, who also possessed a
barren womb, *"Though your body may
be barren your mind is not."*
From the time Valerie first
learned to read, she read whatever
she could. As she surmised, the
activity kept her sane in her
solitude.
****
Alecksander reined his feisty
stallion in at Smithton's limits
and perused the colony. His
horse's shiny deep black dappled
coat glistened with the sweat of
its spirited temperament.

He ran one of his hands down the animal's right-hand shoulder to calm it. The horse snorted and shook its head, but stilled at the authority of the great man's suggestion.

The resolved rider then released the tension he held on the reins. At its freedom, his nimble horse continued on his way to their next destination.

Alecksander looked over the township as they entered and took in a deep inhalation. *I do not ken wherefore this township be my next objective.*

An inescapable enticement, which drew him to Smithton, seemed the only thing he did know. It appeared the town, or something in it, awaited him.

****

Valerie treasured her emotional talent for deep compassion in spite of all the risks involved. It came by her while she cared for the sick aboard the ship she'd traveled on to the new land.

She remembered her life as a child on-board the ship. Most of her memories came back to her as happy ones, except for her parents' tragic deaths.

Another family soon took her in. When the ship arrived at the new world, the family made their home in Massachusetts. Valerie remained there until adulthood.

Valerie attended school because in the state of Massachusetts, settlements of at least 50 families were mandated to support schools.

Even though children attended at separate hours due to their different sexes, both boys and girls attended the "common schools." Her ability to heal others emotionally made Valerie different from the others; so she avidly learned to read and write.

Valerie sometimes fretted over the deaths in her life. *I don't ken wherefore I survived the passage and my mother and father didn't.* She only knew her emotions formed a deep connection with those who fell sick during that long and arduous journey.

When the colonists first arrived, they sought Valerie out for her newfound wisdom. She helped those who suffered from "demons" in their heads.

But later, the colonists shied away from her out of fear *because* of her mysterious ability.

On their later recognition of her
barren body, she was shunned for
it too.
Now, the settlers only
approached her if in dire need of
her assistance with their
children. Other than that,
Valerie lived in solitude until
her services were called upon.
Valerie's unique talent
became especially valued to her
once she achieved adulthood and
learned of her barrenness. Her
prized ways enabled her to share
the feelings and emotions of the
abused and unhappy children
wherever she went. They enabled
her to love and care for the young
ones as if they were her own.
Valerie reflected on how her
ways of caring for others came to
mind more often since the rumors
began. The stories, which arrived
from Europe, told of something
called witches and their evil
practices.
The spread of the stories
from the old continent via the
ships didn't take long.
Originally, the colonists clamored
for her attention to their
disturbed children. Now they
didn't.

The gossip never gave Valerie
any peace. *My life 'tis changed
forever.* Anxious stories from
abroad caused an over amount of
panic amongst the settlers in the
new world.
Colonial fingers pointed at
the least popular among them. The
accusations aimed at Valerie, too.
Now only those younger colonists
with the most severe personality
disorders came to see her.
*'Tis as if I have magical
powers or the like of such. Most
certes I be not a witch.*

Chapter Six

Chatter from children outside
Valerie's unfinished cottage
jerked her from her opinions about
witches. She stilled her hands on
the blouse she mended and listened
in.
She widened her eyes and held
her breath when the voices told
her about a witch hunter who'd
arrived.
Valerie's heart pitched
upward and the nerves on the top
of her head scattered. *A witch
hunter hath never come to Smithton
before.*
Valerie's anxious heart
squeezed. She held her sewing
needle between the fingers of each
hand and stretched it out between
them. Worrisome thoughts
cluttered in her mind.

'Tis only a children's game.
Her thought of reassurance pushed
any possible concept of doom from
her mind. She grasped what
comfort it gave and resumed her
sewing. Her attention to the
children outside ceased.

****

Alecksander pulled back on
the reins, and stopped his horse
near a crude cottage. A group of
children played at its porch.
*'Tis the aura about this place
attracts me here.*
He stretched his long legs in
the stirrups. His motion
straightened him in the saddle,
from where he scrutinized the
mostly unsettled landscape around
him.
*There must be something I
recognize here.* He examined
everything in eyesight, but knew
he couldn't recognize a
familiarity with anything.
A tortured flash of déjà vu
disagreed with him. The distant
memory informed him he did know
about this place. Nervous
disquiet riddled his body.
Reliance on reason told him
the humble abode reminded him of
others he'd seen, coincidence. He
shook his head. The great

Alecksander didn't believe in chance.

A mystery remains to be solved here. I must investigate.

Alecksander dismounted near the active children and dropped his horse's reins. He crossed his arms, balanced on legs angled out in an upended Vee, and perused the children.

His horse also waited in silence, ears alert, as if he paid attention to the scene in front of him, too, but Penumbra remained ground-tied where Alecksander left him.

The children immediately stopped and stared at the stranger. The rocks they tossed dropped and their games ceased. They clustered together and the biggest little boy stepped toward Alecksander.

The boy crossed his arms across his chest in a defiant male pose, cleared his throat and said, "We've not seen ye here afore now. Be ye the witch hunter we hear travels our land?"

Alecksander stared at the boy. *How do they ken the direction of my travels? I announce my paths to none.* He straightened his full five foot

eleven inches into an erect pose
he knew would intimidate them.

In his own bold show, the
witch hunter glowered down on the
young one whom he assumed to be
all of about six or seven years
old. He demanded, "'Tis wherefore
ye ask?"

All the bravado vanished from
the young one who stared up into
the threat of his dark eyes. It
amused Alecksander, though he made
no show of it.

The little boy's shoulders
fell and his skinny arms dropped
down to his sides. He swallowed
hard as if in wonder of what he
should say next.

The child took a quick back-
glance. It seemed he looked for
backup. The group of children
behind him shrugged their
shoulders. At their lack of
support; he returned his attention
to the man.

By his vacant expression; it
appeared the child dove back into
the eyes that scowled down on him.
With his attention locked to
Alecksander's gaze, he drew an
arch in the dirt with one of his
feet. "Just wonderin'."

"I am," Alecksander stated in
answer to the original question.

He opened his mouth to ask, but then closed it in belief the boy didn't need to know about his curiosity as to how they knew he'd come.

"Now, be gone with ye," he added with a broad sweep of his arm to point in the opposite direction. All of ye!" He grinned when the children shrieked and ran off.

His moment of gratification in his foreboding action soon vanished. He returned the serious nature to his expression when he again looked on the humble abode. *Mayhap a witch be here.*

****

The children's shrieks, and the sudden silence, again drew Valerie out of her reverie. *Be it now?* She put her materials to her side, went to her door, and opened it.

her lower abdomen tickled at the sight of the man who stood before her. Valerie didn't know how, but she knew the person who stood outside her door. *Who is he?*

Chapter Seven

Valerie placed the fingers of one hand to the side of her forehead. It lightened in the hazy sensation of a faint. She swallowed the discomfort of foreknowledge away.

I've never swooned at the sight of a man afore, and I shan't begin now. She refocused her visitor. *Whatever bothers me couldn't be this stranger at my door.*

"May I help ye, sir?" she asked in a tremulous query.

The man at her door looked about himself, into her home, and back again to her face. He appeared as curious as she about the reason he stood there.

She took a quick peek around him, but saw no children anywhere. A state of sudden breathlessness swooped up through her. *What has he done with the children?*

Her heart skipped, but she didn't know if it did so in fear of what became of the boys and girls, or attraction to this man whose magnetism struck her hormones in a sinful way.

I most certes do not ken this man. But somehow she knew she did, used to, or wanted to know him very well. *Seems so right he be at my door.*

Valerie's emotions dizzied her, but she wouldn't give in to them. She gave a moment of silent thanks when the unfamiliar person at her door broke the uncomfortable silence.

He made a sweeping bow and introduced himself, "Greetings, ma'am. I be Alecksander Stone. I stopped here...." He touched his temple with one of his index fingers.

Valerie took note of the possible significance in his pause. *Of what does he wonder in this awkward moment?*

"....Um, to water my horse at thy well," he quickly finished.

Valerie smiled and gathered her skirt in a small curtsey. "'Tis an honor to meet ye, sir.

My name be Valerie Baldwin. The water for which ye search, 'tis over there."

She pointed to the small stream, which by-passed her property. "Did ye not see it?" she asked. She eyed him with suspicion and wondered at the real reason for his visit.

I need to ken more about this man. She snatched her day shawl from the wall post by the door as she followed him and his horse to the stream.

"Verily, 'tis thy business here?" Valerie asked after him. Alecksander didn't answer. His lack of response irked her. At the stream, his horse stretched its neck to drink.

He paused beside his animal and stroked its shoulder blade for a minute before he returned his attention to Valerie. "Thank ye for the water, ma'am.

"Tis correct ye be with thy guess the water be not the reason for my visit. I'll not bother ye for long. I pass through in search of another job."

Excitement leaped through Valerie with thoughts of the jobs she needed done on her home. "'Tis the job ye 'search' for?"

Once more the man stood silent. It seemed as if he considered his next words. "I'm, um, a hunter, ma'am." The pain of mortal fear shot through Valerie's body.

She opened her mouth, but didn't have time to ask for what he hunted before he spoke again. "How do ye make thy livelihood, ma'am?"

"How be it I live?" she answered with a question. Not at all certain of what she'd say, she widened her eyes and stuttered, "I-I be a healer."

His gaze traveled over her property. "I don't see any menfolk around. Do ye live here alone?"

Valerie felt the need to especially consider her next words. *I do not want him to think me too vulnerable.* "Mayhap sometimes, but oftentimes not."

She strengthened her voice in a rush of renewed self-confidence. *I have no need be afraid of this man.*

"I have no worries of living my life here alone. The nearby village folk be good. They be at my side at a moment's notice if I give a distressed call to them."

Valerie lowered her eyes in a moment of contrition. So she'd stretched the truth a bit. She did know her native friends would assist her in time of need. *He doesn't need to ken that.*

Alecksander stretched his long lean body up toward the sky in a full body extension and yawned. He appeared if no longer interested in her words.

Valerie's nature to nurture rose to the fore at his tired action. "Ye be riding for long?"

He nodded. "Since early morning, ma'am."

She glanced at the mid-day sun. "Would ye care to rest a minute, here?"

"Thank ye, ma'am. A few moments of rest would agree with me." He stretched out on his side on the ground. His horse's reins dangled beside him.

Alecksander positioned his long legs so one lay straightened and the other bent up at the knee. His upper body lay supported by an upper arm on an elbow from where he kept watch on her.

Valerie experienced fits as she argued with herself. *He can lay here in front of my home and*

47

*rest for a bit. But that ground's
so hard!*

She had no idea why she felt
the need to comfort him, but she
did. Her emotions twisted in
turmoil as her vision flicked back
and forth between him and her
cottage.

The wild berries her new
friends gave her to brew returned
to her mind. The natives called
the tea "sumacade." She always
kept a supply brewed. *I should
offer him a drink.*

Her returned attention to her
visitor showed his once rapt
observation of her ceased. He now
fiddled with some twigs. "Would
ye care for an afternoon
accompaniment to thy day's
travels? Mayhap some tea?"

He gathered his long limbs
under him and stood. "Thank ye
much, ma'am. I would, if 'tis not
a bother."

Valerie retraced her steps
between him and her home. The
sound of his footsteps gave his
track of her away. She turned
toward him with one of her hands
held up. "Ye don't need to
follow. I can bring it out to
ye."

His response came quick, "I have already caused ye enough trouble, ma'am. I can at least save ye the trip to and from thy cottage on my account."

Valerie turned and continued on. This time, she didn't comment when he followed. Inexplicably, the circumstance of her solitude with a man she didn't know, no longer alarmed her.

Valerie's scalp tingled for a reason she couldn't figure when the man stopped. The sadness of a great loss washed over her. Without a cease in her steps she invited him in. "Ye may join me inside."

Her heart jumped and she froze in sudden astonishment at her brazenness the instant she stepped over the threshold. *Wherefore did I do that? Hath I gone crazy?*

Chapter Eight

Alecksander stopped at the bottom of her porch steps. He waited there as she walked inside for the tea. His ears tingled. His skin tightened.

He sensed each hair on his neck as it rose. All his senses forewarned him before he stepped up onto her porch, but of what he didn't know.

Though his body's inexplicable reaction should have disturbed him, it didn't. Instead, it soothed his emotions and intrigued him to follow.

He massaged his chin and questioned his instincts. *"Tis wise I follow her in?* His mind entertained forbidden thoughts.

He glanced downward. It seemed the earth at his feet mired them. His body gave an inward shiver with the puzzlements his subconscious harbored.

He gave a glance downward. It seemed the earth at his feet mired them. His body gave an inward shiver with the puzzlements his subconscious harbored.

Wherefore did I expect her invitation? She doesn't ken me; does she? I've seen her. I ken that. Whence have I seen this beautiful woman afore? What spell 'tis she toils?

Miss Valerie's appearance beckoned him. Her well-rounded figure enticed him. The long fiery brunette hair, which curled around her face, set off her creamy complexion.

In spite of his hormonal reaction, the mystical powers he possessed told him her inner spirit called out to him most. *Of that I must beware.*

Another inward shudder racked him at his cognizance. An honest beauty such as she, had never affected him in that way before. They tried to attract him, but he held no interest.

The only women who attracted him in this way before were the witches he hunted, and he knew the difference. They attracted him with the falsehoods of their outer beauty, not with their genuine beauty from within.

This woman attracted him with both her inner and outer beauty. But she could still be a witch. *I must discern what 'tis she holds over me.*

Alecksander admitted, albeit with reluctance, this Valerie woman attracted him in an extremely intimate way. He knew he'd searched for a woman such as her, but not in the same way he looked for the *others*.

His soul connected with hers in a way never before experienced by him. *That aspect stands between me and my discrimination of her ways. I cannot be deceived by that.*

Alecksander needed to know the truth. The doers of evil all looked out for him. At every turn in each witch-hunt he performed, the practitioners of witchery strove to affect him.

He focused on the woman in the cottage. *'Tis a trick? Be she a witch?* He didn't want to believe that — not of her.

Questions tormented the self-assured witch hunter. *Could she indeed be a witch who has cast her*

*spell on me during an unguarded
moment? Could it be wherefore she
affects me the way she does?*
Those of the craft always
attracted him to their locations,
just as he felt Miss Valerie
attracted him to her home. Only
one logical explanation remained.
He surrendered to the verdict
without enthusiasm. *She be a
witch. I must watch her, and
myself.* He then took a firm self-
assured stride into her home.

* * * *

Valerie's nerves thrilled
when he entered. He strode in
like he owned the place.
Although, his apparent attitude
didn't disturb her as much as it
ought.
By his expression, it seemed
he harbored innate curiosity about
his surroundings. He appeared
familiar with them, but not.   His
demeanor aroused her suspicions.
His intent focus appeared
centered on Valerie. Intimate
tickles stirred through her with
thoughts of their intended unity.
*I be his; he be mine. We belong
always together.*
The visions sent to her mind
from deep within her hormonal
center bewildered and set her

53

insides queasy. Her head took a
momentary tic.
　　'*Tis like déjà vu. From
whence does this sensation come?
'Tis most queer.* She broke their
gaze and regained her composure
with an inward shudder.
＊＊＊
　　Alecksander knew her
deliberation when she broke their
gaze. He took special note of her
unconscious behaviour and
remembered his original mission.
　　When his heart nagged at him
about what would happen if he
found her to be a witch, he sent
it a cold reminder. '*Tis my
position. The woman called me
here.*
　　*She be nothing to me. 'Tis
none of my business what they do
to their own after my revelations.*
　　Her obvious and deliberate
straightened posture betrayed to
him one thing, and brought on more
questions. *She be nervous about
something.*
　　*What be it she hides? What
kind of "healer" be she?* He hoped
he wouldn't need to turn her in.
Alecksander's true desire would be
he found her genuine, like him.
　　He drank his tea down with a
last couple of gulps and clapped

54

his empty pewter mug on her table
with a soft thud. "Thank ye for
the drink, ma'am. I must go now."
He stood, touched the tip of
his tri-cornered hat in salute
before he replaced it on his hand,
and turned toward where his horse
waited outside.

Chapter Nine

Valerie watched as Alecksander gained the saddle. The man's indifferent mannerisms told her he didn't want to see or know any more about her or her place of existence.

His horse pranced in place and he tossed over his shoulder before he set onto the trail, "I must see to business in the township."

She swallowed her pride at his cold attitude and touched the sides of her skirt in an implied curtsey. *That be rather quick. Why does he seem so hurried to get away?*

Adrenalin lifted her heart. *I never got a chance to ask him for what 'tis he hunts!* She ran out to catch the horseman before

he left, with her skirt bundled up
in her hands.

"Wait! I need to ask!"

He directed his curious
vision down to her from on his
animal's lean muscled back. "Need
to ask?"

Valerie halted at the horse's
side, out of breath from her
agitated pace. She looked up to
him. One of her palms landed on
her breast while she caught her
breath. "For what 'tis ye hunt,"
she panted.

"I hunt for . . . things."

Every nerve in Valerie's body
alerted at his paused answer. She
heated and shivered at the same
time. *I cannot allow him to see
the effect he has on me.*

With that thought, Valerie
swallowed her edginess. She
cocked her head to portray an
innocent air of curiosity and
asked him, "Things?"

"Things such as a lovely
young woman as ye should have no
need to give thought to." His
quick explanation did little to
answer her question.

Valerie's spine stiffened as
she fought back a moment of
indignation. *So he thinks to*

presume his knowledge of what I should 'give thought to'.

Their conversation ended when he turned his horse away from her. Then, as if given another reason to delay, he turned his anxious mount back to her.

"I would like to come back and call on ye again, under different circumstances, if that be to ye liking?"

Valerie gave her head a slight nod. Her heart warmed as she watched Alecksander ride away. *'Tis the first person who has come to visit with me in a long time, and he wants to return to "call on" me.*

She smoothed her hair. *I hope I didn't appear too eager for his return.* She'd given up on the hope of a man in her life after her former husband and his mistreatment. *Mayhap that will change!* Of course, she knew it would take a miracle.

After he kens my divorced status and inability to bear children, he too might not want to spend an over amount of time with me. He also might not understand how my unusual abilities are not related to witchery.

I must be careful when and with what I tell him. The next realization she encountered covered her skin with a rash of tiny shivers. *He didn't tell me for what 'tis he 'hunts.'*

★★★★

Alecksander warmed inside at Miss Valerie's blush when she'd smiled at him and nodded. He'd returned her smile and gave leave to his ready horse. *She needn't ken for what 'tis I hunt.*

The village limits of Smithton stood within sight and wouldn't take but a short time for him to reach. Even so, dust flew as his horse carried him off at a run.

I need to get away from her. It would do no good if he dared remain and allowed his questions about her, or her questions about him, to grow.

Alecksander barreled into town with the speed of a small tornado. By their visible reactions, he imagined his rapid entry into Smithton shocked township's society.

Each colonist on the main road stepped back and stared at him. Tied horses shied. Drivers

on the road fought to control
their lead animals.

When Alecksander pulled up on
his reins, his horse skidded to a
stop in front of the salon. He
swung his long legs down and noted
his horse lathered from its mouth
and glistened with sweat.

He gave his horse's left
shoulder a stroke after he
dismounted, and tied it to an
unoccupied hitching post before he
left it. His animal trembled in
his wake.

Alecksander paused after a
couple of steps and straightened
his long black cloak about his
shoulders. He paid no attention
to the townsfolk who still gawked
at him.

When he entered the meeting
place, he saw six seated
gentlemen. Some others milled
about. The witch hunter reasoned
they'd only recently arrived; most
of those present still wore their
cloaks.

They all appeared unaware of
his entrance. Those present drank
and visited. Alecksander
envisioned a small crowd of
colonists would soon gather.

The Smithton elders quieted.
They looked up at his entrance. A

man seated behind a table at the head of the room pushed his stool back with a loud scrape on the floor.

The authoritative man rose and pounded on the table with his fist. "Sir! State thy name and business."

"Alecksander Stone. Just passing through."

The elder who spoke gave rise to indignation, "This be a place of township business. 'Tis not a place for a stranger. The *public* salon be down the road."

Unbothered by the man's tone, Alecksander removed the tri-corner hat from his head of shoulder-length near-black hair. "I thought I might find a drink in *this* place."

The men at the table engaged in a moment of muffled discussion. The original speaker inquired of him in a much more respectful tone, "Ye be the renowned Alecksander Stone, Hunter of Witches Extraordinaire?"

Alecksander nodded his head in a self-conscious air of superiority.

The elder inhaled a deep breath. "May we ask what brings ye here?"

"I pass through, as I saith."

The man at the head of the table cleared his throat and dared to ask yet another question of the famed witch hunter, "Have ye heard the talk?"

"Has someone sent for ye?" a man at the first speaker's side blurted without time for a breath.

Chapter Ten

The first speaker soon filled him in, "Children here have become changelings. 'Tis considered a witch be among us!"

The witch hunter's ears perked toward the conversation. "How be ye young ones afflicted?" he asked.

"'Tis an unknown medical condition. The doctor who travels in these parts kens no cure."

"Do ye ken another healer?" Alecksander queried as thoughts of the voluptuous beauty whose cottage he recently visited filled his thoughts.

If Smithton's other healer be Miss Valerie, and if she indeed be a witch, then 'tis sure her spell be cast over me already.

Alecksander swallowed hard. *Never before have I experienced such an attraction to one I hunt.* He noticed his casual question caught everyone's attention.

"Another 'healer'?" they echoed in chorus.

"Yes. Another who might be able to cure ye changelings?"

"Wherefore would ye ask about another 'healer'?" the original magistrate asked. "They be not common."

The question didn't catch Alecksander off-guard. "I happened upon a young woman who professed to be Smithton's healer, whilst on my way to thy village. 'Tis not true?"

The magistrate swallowed hard and gave him a solemn nod. "Yes. 'Tis there she lives. We in this community be cautious of this woman in the past weeks."

Alecksander raised an eyebrow in query.

The officer at the head of the table answered the question he saw on Alecksander's face, "The woman ye happened upon on the far end of this township be a disgraced woman.

"In spite of that, she be somehow taken into the trust of the local matrons, which we have allowed," he stated in reference to the room's total male population.

"She cares for our changelings when the doctor who travels from village to village be unable to. 'Tis that woman we suspect. She shows a special ability with the changelings."

"She be a witch! I tell ye!" an excited council member proclaimed.

The lead man shushed him with a wave of his hand.

"Our children didn't take real sick in their heads until she began to consort with them!" another agitated member of the gathered group added.

"We've warned our womenfolk against confiding our children's troubles to her!" another gentleman proclaimed. "And now the children suffer and become changelings!"

The elder who first spoke to Alecksander nodded in agreement. "We're here today to discuss our next plan of action. If ye are of a like mind; we'd be eager to engage thy services."

Alecksander kneaded his chin contemplation. *On this day I wouldn't agree with them. It could be Miss Valerie be innocent. I'd much rather believe that.*

'Tis better they engage my services than another like me. Mayhap I can lead them away from that young woman. I could point them in another direction. "That could be arranged. What would ye have me do?"

"Find out the truth for us!" they clamored.

"We ken not who or what she be, whether a true healer or a witch. Will ye find that out about her for us?" the main elder roared above the excitement in the room.

Alecksander remained suspicious about why they'd suspect the woman he admired. *Mayhap 'tis a ruse put on by the children involved.*

"I must see and speak with the changelings, before I make my decision on whether it be worth my time, or not."

The magistrate became visibly agitated and threw his hands out to his sides in a fit of passion.

"I can assure ye, Mr. Witch Hunter, 'tis well worth thy time.

"Do ye doubt our apprehensions over the fits the changelings' exhibit?" The portly man cleared his throat, shook his shoulders, and appeared to regain control of himself.

In a more dignified manner of speech, he stated, "We want to take ye to see the changelings, but first we'll wait for the rest of us to arrive. We must *all* vote on this."

The magistrate led Alecksander and the rest of his council to the front door. There they met the colonists whom Alecksander passed on his way into the township.

"Be there not a town meeting in this place at this hour?" the lead gentleman inquired, when all those inside exited the building as he approached.

"Yes there be, and we expect ye. We have with us the Great Alecksander, Witch Hunter Extraordinaire." He placed one of his hands on Alecksander's right shoulder.

Alecksander sent a disdainful glance to the hand on his shoulder.

"This fine man has agreed to help us in our time of need, if we all vote he do so," the council leader lied.

Alecksander raised an eyebrow at the man's supposition, but said nothing.

A clamor arose from those gathered in the street. "We vote so!"

The original elder continued with his story, oblivious to Alecksander's brief expression of disdain, "'Tis good!

"He will now see to our changelings and decide if he agrees with us in our diagnosis of their bewitchment, or not."

The crowd of newcomers nestled around Alecksander's solid form. Hands slapped his shoulders and the settlers all greeted him with joy.

"We welcome ye to Smithton!"

"We greet ye with gratitude!"

Someone tugged on one of his arms. "Come with us! The afflicted changelings be kept on another side of town!"

The voices clamored about him as the citizens pushed to hustle him away.

****

Alecksander balked at their overly-friendly behavior. *This man-handling must stop.* After

their initial push he stood erect
and concentrated.   A protective
aura soon formed about him.
        The crowd moved to his side
and gave him his space as if swept
aside by a long arm. He knew they
moved by a power not their own as
he continued unhampered down the
narrow road.
        Everyone gave way, but he
knew they followed as close behind
as they could while he swept
through town toward his objective.

Chapter Eleven

Disquieted mutters arose from
the colonists who followed
Alecksander. The slow sounds of
their footsteps told him they
followed at a uneasy pace.
   A measured grin creased his
face. Alecksander knew his
presence left them in awe. He
also knew they questioned whether
or not they made the right
decision when they followed.
      The lead council member
eventually stepped ahead of
Alecksander and led the way. "Ye
must follow me," the self-
important man demanded.
   The remainder of the council
took heart and followed closer. A
hush ensued in the air when
Alecksander and their leader
reached the locked cottage where
the changelings were kept.

The witch hunter stepped forward and left the others behind. He continued alone to the closed portal without hesitation to examine the changelings.

It sounded as though a melee occurred behind the door. When he opened it, wails accosted him. The changelings writhed on the floor and acted like madmen. It appeared they competed for Alecksander's attention.

The changelings act as though they are witched. Something evil is upon them. I need to find what, or who, causes their problems.

Although Alecksander still didn't know what tortured the changelings, he knew he'd seen it before in the victims of his previous hunts.

Alecksander stood unfazed by the various antics displayed while he gazed out across the room over the changelings. All the youngsters appeared to be girls.

He made his way to one of the young women and knelt before her. Alecksander looked deep into her eyes in an effort to search out the truth, and asked, "What afflicts ye?"

The motionless girl gazed
back at him with what appeared as
empty eyes. Then she jumped up
and threw her arms out into the
air in a maniacal outburst.

Alecksander remained unfazed
by the child's antic. A woman in
the room rushed to the girl's side
to quiet her. She directed an
accusatory expression at
Alecksander.

He stood and took a calm step
away from the changeling when the
woman shoved between them.

The elder who accompanied the
witch hunter made a quick move to
the intrusive woman. He gripped
her arm and twisted her around to
face him.

"Matron! Do ye not ken who
'tis ye shove aside?"

Like a shade that is drawn,
her expression at once shifted to
one of oppressed obedience. "'Tis
my duty to keep the changelings
calm, sir."

She jabbed a finger toward
Alecksander. "That man sent this
one into fits!"

The magistrate tugged on her
arm and pulled her closer to him.
He spoke to her in a quiet voice,
"'That man' be the Great Witch
Hunter, Alecksander. He has

agreed to give us his opinion of our changelings."

The woman's grey-blue eyes widened and her face reddened. She threw out her arms toward Alecksander and gasped, "I be sorry. I pray thee forgive me, Mr. Alecksander."

The witch hunter nodded, but appeared disinterested. He continued his observances and focused on one child who appeared to be unaffected. Another aspect also surprised him.

In the room he initially assumed only housed girls; this child appeared to be a boy of around ten years. The unchanged young man kept his distance from the changelings.

The boy sat on a corner rush mat just his size. His knees were drawn up. His arms wrapped around them, and his head rested upon them.

The township's elder followed Alecksander's gaze, like a fish to bait, but soon returned his attention on the man. The witch hunter took note of his companion's moment of new focus.

The elder's gaze rested on the boy longer than it took to be noticed. He cleared his throat and explained the boy's presence in the room full of girls.

"'Tis Scotty, orphaned. The boy has no other family. He be here because of his sudden mental withdrawal from our society. The boy be witched."

Alecksander arched a brow in curiosity as the elder continued, "His anti-social behavior began at just the same time as the hysteria and strange actions came from the girls."

Alecksander walked over to the boy, bent his knees to be on a level with the child, and sat on his haunches. "Holla, Scotty."

The boy looked into his face, but said nothing. Alecksander could see much in his little eyes. They weren't empty as the girl's he'd spoken to.

This lad kens something I must hear. "Would ye like to go for a walk with me?"

Scotty widened his soft brown eyes. A hint of a smile graced his lips. He held a small hand out toward Alecksander, who took it gently within his two larger ones.

Alecksander gave Scotty's hand a kind squeeze and said, "Ye wait here. I'll be right back."

He witnessed the boy's smile tug at the corners of his mouth as he stood to walk away.

After a few minutes time with the magistrate, the witch hunter returned to Scotty's side. "Come along, now," the witch hunter said as he held his hand out to Scotty.

The minute they left the building, the boy enlivened and tugged on Alecksander's hand in an effort to run. The man refused to be rushed. He instead directed a solemn gaze down upon the boy. "What be ye hurry, Scotty? Let's remain here a minute." After he didn't hear a word from the child, he again asked, "Tell me, Scotty, what be ye reason to run?"

"We must go!" Scotty said. His little face gained a more earnest expression; he glanced back to the building he'd left, and tugged on Alecksander's hand again with what appeared to be all his might. "Ye must get me away from here! I need to tell her!"

Alecksander kept his face emotionless and blinked back his shock at the sudden coherent words from a boy who hadn't spoken. *I must seize this moment for unanswered questions.*

"Who 'tis ye must tell something to? What must ye tell this person? Wherefore 'tis ye have not spoken to anyone for so long?"

Chapter Twelve

"A witch hunter?" Valerie whispered to herself. She choked on the thought. *Had I imagined that, I would not have gotten so excited he wanted to see me again.*
She held her fingers up and counted on them. It all added up as to how he could be the witch hunter.
He be new here. The changelings do not come to me so often. And now they say a witch hunter hath arrived in Smithton. Her lungs tightened over her held breath. *How could it not be him?*
Her hands broke away from each other and she let one rest on her breast in her panic. Her breath still eluded her. *They punish those suspected of witchcraft with death.*
Visions of reported stake burnings, rock crushings, and

drownings flashed before her mind's eye. *Oh Lord! Those things cannot happen to me.*
, Valerie's heart raced. She fell to her knees on the packed earthen floor of her cottage and hailed the heavens. "Oh, God! I pray thee, help me! Ye ken I be not a witch!"

After a few moments of meditation; she stood with renewed hope and straightened her dress. "Don't be ridiculous, Valerie. Ye have listened to an over amount of the changelings' tales."

Valerie knew she performed magic, but the 'magic' she practiced came from an age-old compassion deep inside her. *My healing doesn't come from supernatural spells.*

Her capabilities were only used to make the lives of children better. Practitioners of witchcraft drove their victims into fits of madness.

KNOCK

The young care-giver jerked up straight to attention at the unexpected knock on her front door. *I wonder who 'tis? I didn't hear the approach of horse hooves.*

She made her way to the door and reached out. The shield between her and whatever waited on its other side screeched, as if it didn't want to be opened.

Valerie girded herself for whom or what she might find on the other side, and tentatively pulled it the rest of the way open.

Her heart melted in relief and her fear vanished when she saw who stood there. She squealed with delight and the excited adrenalin of joy sparked within her soul.

"Scotty! 'Tis ye! I've missed ye! Whence have ye been?" Valerie asked as she sprung through her front door and out onto her porch, arms spread out wide in welcome.

She stumbled to a stop and her chest lurched into her throat when she recognized the man who stood just a few feet away. Her eyes caught his and she stared hard at the supposed witch hunter.

The attractive, quizzical expression she witnessed on his face caused her breath to stop. She protectively gripped Scotty's shoulders, and murmured, "Ye return."

"Yes, I have." The witch hunter glanced down to the boy who stood in front of her. "I hadn't thought to return so quickly, but the boy asked me to bring him here."

She smiled down on the child whose wide smile shone up at her. She saw his body tense before he explained. "I had to get away from there! I had to come and warn ye!"

Her heart stilled in apprehension. "Get away from whence? Warn me about what?" He opened his mouth, but she continued before he had a chance to answer. "I've been so worried about ye. Whence have ye been, honey?"

"They wouldn't let me come back here. They put us all in a cottage by ourselves. They called it a 'qwarntine.'"

Valerie squeezed her eyebrows together. "What do ye mean, 'quarantine'?" *'Tis already a place like Bedlam in Smithton?*

"Rebecca and Elizabeth started acting weird and they blamed it on ye! They saith ye 'charmed' them. Then the elders saith it be witchcraft!"

Valerie inhaled, "Oh." "And are they who ye came to warn me about?"

"No. Him!" the boy sputtered as he pointed back toward Alecksander.

Valerie jerked her head up to look at Alecksander. His presence confused her. *Wherefore in this land of God's Green Creation did Scotty bring the man I need be warned about, with him?*

Scotty tugged on Valerie's skirt and she returned her gaze to him.

"'Twas the only way I could get here!" He stretched up onto his tiptoes, cupped his mouth and whispered to her, "Don't worry; I didn't tell *them* anything, and I tricked *him*."

Valerie raised her eyebrows at his words.

****

Alecksander mimicked her quizzical expression. He couldn't help he overheard Scotty's exuberant whisper. He returned his face to its fixed expression the instant Valerie set her gaze on him.

The ashen shade of her face tugged at a place deep inside him he didn't know existed. *I don't want to scare her.*

He didn't want to find anything out about her either—for *them*, anyway. But he had a job to do. "I asked if I could call on ye," he reminded her.

"Of course. 'Tis wherefore ye be here," she mumbled. Valerie lowered her eyelids as if she hoped he didn't notice her blush.

Alecksander appreciated her demure gesture. *Her blush; 'tis becoming on her.* Valerie looked back to him without a show of embarrassment that he could see.

"Of course. I remember saying ye could call on me," she admitted.

Scotty jerked into an erect posture and questioned her. "Ye already ken him?" he squeaked in astonishment.

She nodded. "Yes, dear. We have met. But I don't really 'ken' him." Her attention returned to Alecksander. "Ye may sit with us. Would ye care for more tea?"

Scotty yanked on her sleeve. "No! I must talk to ye alone." He jabbed an index finger at Alecksander. "Tell *him* to go away from here. He be a witch hunter!"

Valerie shushed the boy. His innocent statement incriminated her. "Do not be rude. The man be a guest. And he brought ye here to me from . . ."

Alecksander took a step back. He imagined she thought the worst. *She must puzzle over where Scotty escaped from with my help.*

"Mayhap 'tis best if I come to call at some other time." There was no need to rush what seemed more inevitable as time passed.

Scotty nodded hard from his spot under Valerie's arm.

Valerie smiled and accepted Alecksander's offer, "Thank ye. Ye be very kind. I have never seen Scotty so upset." She led Scotty away a short distance, and murmured to him, "Be ye sure he hunts for witches?"

Alecksander lied with a straight face when he told her, "I don't."

Valerie appeared taken aback when he answered the question he shouldn't have heard. *I cannot believe this attractive woman be a witch, as those who send me suggest.*

But Alecksander still wondered about her ways. "The boy

won't be missed." Then, without
another word, he mounted his horse
and rode away.

***

*I do not ken wherefore I want
to find him not to be a witch
hunter. How did he ken what I
asked Scotty?* Valerie's heart
plummeted as she watched
Alecksander leave.

But the boy would leave her
no peace. Her balance faltered as
he tugged on her skirt for her
attention.

Scotty pointed after the
figure who retreated away from
them and exclaimed, "He lied.
Verily. The man be a witch
hunter."

"How could ye ken that?"
Valerie murmured from somewhere
far away as she continued to watch
Alecksander's departure.

"The elders in Smithton sent
him here to get ye!"

Chapter Thirteen

Valerie jolted out of her reverie at Scotty's words. Her throat clenched and her heart seized. Dread replaced the warmth of attraction she experienced only moments before.

In spite of her reluctance to believe so, it seemed her fears came true. She fisted her palms. *Wherefore needs must I be so attracted to him?*

She placed her hands on her chest to calm their tremble. "Wherefore would the colonist's do such a thing?" she wondered.

"Those two little girls I don't like started acting like Tom's o' Bedlam and told them a bunch of lies about ye."

Valerie immediately knew to whom he referred - Rebecca and Elizabeth. The girls troubled her

from the beginning. She tried her
best to help them sort through
their problems, but they always
acted out.

Through her efforts; Rebecca
appeared to recover from her
problem, but Elizabeth resisted
her efforts to correct her anti-
social behavior. It seemed as if
she relished the extra attention.
*And now they get that attention in
other ways.*

"Ye cannot allow that man to
come back here," Scotty told her,
his eyes narrowed. "Ye needs must
watch out for him. He wants to
prove ye a witch."

Valerie threw her hands up to
her chest in a devout proclamation
of innocence. "'Tis not true!" *I
cannot believe Alecksander would
be so cruel to me. He wanted to
call on me.*

Scotty hugged Valerie's
thighs and looked up to her. "I
ken ye be not a witch. But when
those two girls got into trouble,
they blamed it on ye so they
wouldn't be punished."

Valerie placed a hand to her
forehead. "Oh dear." She backed
up and sat on a bench in her yard
under a white pine tree. Her
pulse raced.

I needs must take a break.
Too much besets me. She took a
deep breath and patted her lap for
Scotty to join her.

"Well, that's enough about
those girls and what they've been
up to. Tell me whence ye have
been. It sounds quite
adventurous. From whence did ye
escape?"

He tilted his head further
upward and his soft brown eyes
made a straight line of sight into
hers. A lock of his wavy blond
hair fell to rest at the inside
corner of one of his eyes.

She reached out and brushed
his hair aside with a loving
stroke as he talked to her.

"I told ye. The ol' leaders
in Smithton took me and made me
stay in the same place whence
those girls are."

"I pray thee tell me, if ye
didn't act up, wherefore did they
do that?"

The boy skewed his face and
looked at her in the same way he
might regard an idiot. "They
thought I was witched, too."

Valerie cocked her head and
sent him a curious gaze. "But
wherefore? Did ye blame anyone a
witch?"

"No. I wouldn't tell them anything. At first I told them a lot of good things about ye. And I told them how those girls lied, but they didn't believe me, so I just stopped talking.

Then they saith I couldn't talk because I had a spell on me. But they wouldn't believe me when I *did* talk to them!" He trembled with frustration in his excitement.

Valerie hugged him close to her in an effort to comfort him. "Calm down, honey. All will be good." Then she gazed off into the distance where Alecksander rode. *Did he really just happen on my home 'for water'?*

Scotty tugged on her sleeve and once more jerked her from her reverie. Valerie returned her attention to him and scolded, "I pray thee; have patience, young man!"

Immediate tears brimmed in his soulful eyes at her comment. Valerie's heart ached at his hurt appearance, "I be sorry, dear. I didn't mean to snap at ye."

"'Tis good. I don't want ye mad at me. Telling him a story was the only way I could get away to see ye." Along with the stomp of one of his little feet, he urged, "Ye must refuse him, and send him away if he returns."

Valerie simmered. Her head raged with turbulent emotions at the witch hunter's intrusion into her life. Her sentiments argued with a passion she couldn't quite identify. *Wherefore this strong desire?*

She placed one of her hands on the boy's head and again brushed a strand of his soft mid-shoulder-length hair back into place. "I will watch out for myself the best I can," she assured him.

****

Alecksander didn't ride far before he stopped and turned his horse to face the direction from where he came. Reflection filled his mind. *What has that woman done to me?*

"Witchcraft," he mumbled as he wheeled Penumbra around and headed for Smithton. He knew one of his marks of greatness as a witch hunter came by way of his immunity to spells, whereas others of his trade failed.

I must be daft for thinking of her the way I have. A witch hunter has no time for a woman in

his life — especially a witch.
Mayhap the people of Smithton be
right about her.

Chapter Fourteen

Knock! Knock!
Valerie spilled her morning tea at the unexpected firm rap on her door early the next day. She trained her anxious eyes on the entryway. In memory of the last surprise visitor who brought her joy, she lowered her emptied cup to her table and inquired, "Who be it?"

A short answer came back to her. "'Tis Alecksander."

Valerie unconsciously ran her hands over her hair and down the front of her dress on her trip to the doorway. Her rebellious insides tingled deep within her with eager anticipation as she pulled her door open. *I must be sure to not smile.* "What brings ye out so early on this morrow, sir?"

Alecksander arched an eyebrow at her and folded his body into a slight bow. His mannerisms deepened the passionate sensations she experienced for him. "I have returned to call in a proper fashion, as I told ye I would."

Valerie appreciated his smile. *'Tis one in which he appears likewise as happy to see me again as I feel in return.* Her face warmed as the fondness in his expression grew. Scotty's words, *send him away,* echoed in her mind.

Her gut wrenched in indecision. *I want to invite him in to stay for a visit. But can I trust him? Scotty saith I cannot.* The man lied about it being a 'proper' time to call, her moral values reminded her. After quick deliberation, she decided it would be best if her trust remained with Scotty.

Valerie lowered her head before him and replied demurely, "Calls in the early morrow be most improper, sir. 'Tis also most improper if ye call on me in private, as ye do."

As if he'd rehearsed all she might say to him, not a moment passed until Alecksander responded with a proper resolution. "In that case, we should meet in Smithton amongst the colonists."

In an equally quick surprise at his immediate answer, Valerie returned her gaze to him. Once more she found herself greeted by a raised eyebrow—this time along with a playful quirk of his lips. "Shall we?" he asked as he held an arm out to her.

Valerie gazed past him into oblivion and envisioned the way most of the villagers shunned her solitary way of life. But when she gazed back into his playful brown eyes, all was lost. Her femininity yearned for the familiarity her body told her they both possessed.

She did not want to turn him down, but knew she must for her own safety. *Scotty has warned me!* "No," she answered with as blank a face as she could muster. "I think we should not meet at all."

Alecksander cocked his head to her. It appeared her sudden lack of interest surprised him, as if he couldn't imagine why she wouldn't want to be escorted into Smithton on his arm.

"I be sorry, ma'am. I assumed thy interest in my company when I first came here. Wherefore would ye decide we should not meet?" he asked, with what sounded like his best 'poor me' tone of voice.

Valerie warmed as her blush deepened. "Well, sir, I just do not think we should." Her heart pitter-patted against the inside of her chest as she imagined what she should say next. *I cannot tell him my rejection of his offer be because he thinks me a witch.*

She sighed with her dilemma. "As I saith earlier, 'twould not look right to have a man come to call on a single woman who lives alone. I also do not think we should go into town together." *There be enough rumors about me as 'tis.*

Another flirtatious quirk of his eyebrow tickled her in the most intimate ways and places. "Think about it, will ye?" He lowered his arm and without another word, climbed onto his horse. The animal began a slow trot and he rode away on it with a great show of nonchalance.

"Huzzah!" Scotty called out from behind her.

Valerie started in her remembrance of his night spent with her. One of her hands went

to her chest as she turned to him.
"Ye scared me!" She delighted in
his impish grin. "I verily forgot
ye were here."

"Tis good ye sent him away,"
Scotty replied.

She did her best to dispel
her attraction to the man who left
her, by devoting her full
attention to Scotty. "Come. I
have some fresh vegetables I have
stewed. We can have them for
breakfast this morning."

"Pray pardon me," Scotty
asked of Valerie when he finished
his meal.

She smiled and nodded at his
proper use of a young man's
etiquette. "Ye may go outside to
play now." He jumped up and
scooted out the back way, *yet
still a boy.* She continued to
smile as she cleared and washed
their breakfast dishes.

When finished with her chore,
Valerie wandered outside to see
what antic her little charge could
be engaged in. She needed not
look very far to find him. The
boy sat on the ground in silence
and busily sketched a picture in
the sand with a twig.

Valerie took a quiet seat on a bench nearby and let him be. *It will be best if I allow him to draw out his thoughts and we can discuss them.*

Scotty looked up at her with eyes that again held a glimmer of tears when he finished his picture.

"What be wrong this time, Scotty?" She glanced over her shoulder in the direction Alecksander had ridden. "Could thy current unhappiness have more to do with that man who called early this morrow?"

He nodded his head violently several times. "Yes. I be afraid. That man be bad! Ye like him, don't ye?"

Valerie rubbed one of her palms over the back of the other, and then cupped her fingers together. "Well, I . . ."

"Verily!" the agitated child cut in. "Ye are going to see him again, aren't ye?"

Valerie opened her arms to him, and Scotty drifted into them. She lifted him onto her lap.

"I might. I do not ken," she answered with a tone of complete wonder at herself and what she might do. In a quick change of

96

subject, she looked down and asked, "What have ye drawn there?" Scotty looked down to his artwork displayed in the dirt. It comprised a burst of lines that, like fireworks, emanated in all directions.

The picture caught her by surprise. There had been no such explosive displays there. *He must have seen fireworks in old world celebrations*. On closer examination, she realized the squiggles actually appeared to be the sparks of a bonfire.

"'Tis a burning," the child murmured.

"A *burning*? Wherefore would ye draw that?"

""That be what scares me most."

Valerie leaned down and took a closer examination of the scratches on the ground, before she said anything else. She pointed at a visage she imagined she saw. "'Tis a face?" she asked. There be someone in that fire?"

"Yes."

Her insides quivered. "Wherefore would ye draw someone in the fire? Who be it?"

He squirmed. She calmed him with her embrace, and he sobbed out, "It . . . it be ye, Miss Valerie."

The quiver inside her stilled, followed by a chill. She tightened her arms around him as if her life depended on it, but did not look at him directly when she quietly asked, "Wherefore would ye draw a picture of me in a fire?"

"Th-that man who was h-here wants to see ye b-burn," he blubbered.

Valerie's heart sank into her lungs and her breath caught on it in pain. "Oh. . . I see." She rubbed her cheek on the top of Scotty's head and continued her squeeze on him. In an effort to console him, she sought to comfort herself too, "Do not worry. That will not happen. They only burn witches."

Scotty stiffened in her arms and exclaimed, "I told ye, he wants to prove ye a witch!"

Chapter Fifteen

Valerie's mind squeezed into a headache of fear. "Be ye sure he wants to prove me a witch?" she asked the boy with as much composure as she could.

"Yes! I told ye about those two bad girls. Because of them, the whole town thinks ye a witch. That one, who wouldn't talk until after she saw ye, told them ye did a spell on her and made her talk. Her parents told everyone ye charmed her." He took a breath only after his speech ended.

Valerie remembered how she helped Rebecca overcome her fear of speaking. The colonists—and a lot of other things— frightened the poor child. The cause for the girl's paranoia stayed hidden from Valerie during the all-too-brief time they spent together.

Her ability to share Rebecca's fears and show them as harmless enabled Valerie to entice the girl to speak. The "miracle" excited her parents about her toils with their changeling. She did no witchery. Her parents gave no indication they suspected her of witchcraft, then. *But why do they now?*

Valerie's internal disquiet broke when a bird flapped in a nearby tree. She glanced up to see what kind it could be, but did not detect the sound's instigator. Regardless, the solitary pine held her gaze and her mind took to wander again in review of the information Scotty offered.

After a bit she looked down to the child, who'd since slid off her lap, and saw he recommenced his etches in the sand. Valerie continued her conversation with him as if there had been no pause.

"I thought those girls loved me."

"I thought so, too." Scotty's immediate response startled her. "I guess they decided they didn't love ye after all."

Valerie accepted his warmth and melted into his embrace when he jumped up and threw his arms around her.

"But I didn't act out, because I still love ye!" She noticed his moistened eyes held real tears at this time. "I did not lie. I did not tell them anything bad about ye."

Now Valerie knew she could no longer deny it. She needed to present her case to the magistrate and his council to explain her situation to them. She needed to stress she did not practice witchcraft. The only thing she did practice was her love for children.

I needs must be sure they understand I would never do anything to hurt the young ones.

After a deep breath, she remembered Scotty's worry and made a verbal affirmation to the child. "I will never allow that witch hunter to come near me again."

When Scotty appeared quite satisfied with her words, she squeezed one of his hands.

"Everything will be all right, Scotty, ye will see. I needs must first clear things up with each of the parents and with the town council, and all will be fine."

She tapped the tip of his upturned nose with one of her fingers. "Ye need not be afeared any longer. I promise ye, thy word is good with me. I will not allow that man to come around me anymore."

Suddenly a frown appeared on Scotty's face as he looked up at her. His lower lip trembled. His eyes once more moistened and his whole body vibrated with emotion, but he said nothing.

Valerie cupped his expressive little face in her hands. *This little one always thinks.* She did not know what else she could say to calm him. *My dear child, I wish ye would not be afeared, because I ken I am.*

Valerie debated with herself throughout the afternoon over what would be best for her little friend during this time. After much consideration, she decided she should call on her native friends. They would provide a safe haven for Scotty.

"Scotty! 'Tis time for ye to come inside now," Valerie called from her front door as he played in the trees outside. The sun sat just above the horizon. Valerie held a hand over her brow and turned her head back and forth when he did not run from his forest haven to her.

She could not see the child anywhere. Her heart picked up into an erratic beat until tree branches crackled and alerted her. He slid down a nearby tree's trunk with ease, as if on an icy stick.

"There ye be!" The boy ran to the door where she stood. Valerie shook her finger in his face and scowled at him. "Ye scared me when I did not see ye!"

"I be sorry," he apologized.

Valerie smiled at his mischievous manner. "Never ye mind. Do not do that to me again," she scolded as she took Scotty into her cottage.

A cup of hot cocoa, which she hoped would lull him into an early bedtime, waited for him on her kitchen counter. She took the warm drink to her chair-side table and invited Scotty onto her lap to drink it while she sat with him in her rocking chair.

The boy drank it in a matter of minutes. Then, with no words said, they rocked together in content until he cuddled up into her arms and fell into a deep sleep.

'Tis time I put my plan into action. She bundled him into her bed and left him where she knew he would be safe, while she took a short trip to the nearby Wampanoag village.

Her indigenous friends acknowledged her presence without visible notice, yet she knew they welcomed her. In their easy way of pleasant nods and smiles, the acceptance of their congenial camp absorbed her.

The village's everyday activities calmed Valerie's soul. Some women busied themselves with cooking, while others stitched deerskin clothing, and still others wove baskets. Men worked on their weaponry, tended to the animals, visited and boasted with each other. Some spoke to her, although she didn't understand all they said.

Kitchi approached and greeted her, "Good day, Val-er-ie!" She smiled when she heard him. *He does verily well with my language.*

Whenever he'd visited her since they'd first met, she coached him in the English language, and her new acquaintance

likewise instructed her in his
native words, which enabled them
to understand each other most
times. His fluent words today
surprised her. She didn't know
any more than their casual words.

Chapter Sixteen

"Good day to ye, Kitchi! I have a favor to ask of ye and thy tribe. May I see thy chief?" Her native friend took the hand she offered to him, and signaled for her to walk with him.

Along the way, they saw some native children who played a game with rocks they tossed amongst each other. With squeals of delight, they waved at her.

Valerie waved and turned her attention back to Kitchi, who led her across the camp. She cast nervous glances about, and followed him in trepidation.

Never before had she ventured this far into the Wampanoag camp— probably because she'd never had a reason to talk to the chief. Her new native acquaintances usually visited her at her home.

They passed several small, round, dome-shaped home sites made of bent and arched saplings. Tree bark covered the abodes in a semblance of weather proofing.

Vapors from an inside fire's smoke curled from a hole cut into the roofs of some, while others appeared to have no fire. It didn't take long before they came to a larger wigwam in the center of the camp.

Kitchi pointed to the dwelling Valerie saw and said, "Sachem."

"Thy chief lives there?" she asked.

"Yes. Go, see Sachem," her friend directed.

Just then, the Wampanoag Sachem stepped out from under a leather door flap from his home. The sight of him took her breath away. Purple shells and beads made from a substance she did not recognize, decorated his deerskin loin cloth.

Eagle feathers cascaded down the back of his head in a single centered row. She appreciated the intricate workings of quills and beads that decorated the base of the article. The sight of its beauty dropped her jaw.

Kitchi's Sachem carried a sharp stone-tipped spear in front of him. A similar tomahawk hung from his side. Still taken aback by his presence, Valerie did not move. She wondered at the formality of his dress. *I hope he's not on his way out somewhere.*

Kitchi walked to his chief's side and spoke to him. The Sachem looked at her and said more words she could not understand. He then lowered his weaponry to the ground.

Her native friend waved her over. "Come. He says, 'Welcome.'"

"Do I interrupt? Is he on his way out?"

"There is always time for a visitor."

"I Thank ye so much," Valerie told the Sachem as she and her friend left his wigwam at the end of their visit. She didn't know how she should speak her thanks in his native Wôpanâak, so she simply gave him a warm smile and a big hug.

Kitchi translated her words and actions. They exchanged smiles and nods and went on their ways.

The sun no longer sat on the
horizon, and Valerie hurried home
for Scotty. It relieved her when
she found him still in a sound
sleep. By appearance; it seemed
Hh did not even miss her. She
wouldn't disturb him, but would
give him the news on the morrow.

Valerie awoke early the next
morning and prepared roasted
vegetables and fish for her and
Scotty to break their fast. It
didn't take long before he joined
her.
"Good morrow, Miss Valerie."
"Good morrow, Scotty." She
smiled at his mannerism while he
wiped sleep from his eyes. "I
have food ready for us to eat and
I also have some news for ye!"
Scotty's eyes widened at the
same time as his smile. "I pray
thee 'tis?"
"Ye like it at the village of
our native friends don't ye?" she
asked him.
"Yes, ye ken I do. Those
people be my friends," he replied.
"I ken I need not ask ye. I
just needed to be sure. I have
made arrangements for ye to stay
in the Wampanoag village with thy
friends until I return for ye."

"Until ye return?" his smile faded to a twisted line of confusion.

"Ye ken I have important business to take care of in Smithton."

The confusion on his face turned into a stark expression of fear. "With that witch hunter man?"

She gave a slow nod. "Yes, with him and all the settlers in Smithton. Whilst I am gone, ye will stay with our friends there where ye will be safe."

Scotty stiffened his little body and his face reddened. He stomped one of his feet and told her exactly what he thought of her plan, "Ye cannot go there alone. I will not allow ye to do it! Ye will be hurt! Those mean people in the township want to burn ye. I needs must go with ye to protect ye."

Valerie felt her insides go cold. She deadened inside with fear at the thought of being burned, but fought the panic and did her best to hide it from Scotty.

"I ken ye believe that, Scotty." *I hope ye be wrong. I pray it not be true.* "Mayhap I

should not go there alone," she
continued, "but I cannot take *ye*
there with me. It might not be
safe for ye in the township,
either. I need to ken ye be safe
while I make things right."

Scotty grabbed her arms, the
hands of which rested on his
shoulders. "I do not want to stay
there!" he shouted. "Do not leave
me there. Ye need me to protect
ye."

"No, Scotty. I believe 'tis
better ye visit with our native
friends. Do not worry about me.
I will be fine. I will explain
everything to the magistrate, and
he will ken." *Verily he will
believe me and they will do me no
harm.*

Valerie stayed up until late
that night. Her heart ached when
she left Scotty behind at the
Wampanoag village that afternoon.
But the thought of his possible
burning as a witch himself because
of his relationship with her, hurt
worse. He would be safe there.

As the night grew deeper,
Valerie paced the floor and peered
out the windows. Her heart raced
and she broke into a cold sweat.
Try as she might, Valerie couldn't

set her mind at rest about the day
that approached. She imagined and
went over and over what she would
           say the next day.
        The night wore on, but she
didn't reach satisfaction with her
words even after the hours she'd
rehearsed. What would she say to
    the magistrate on the morrow?
        Her chest jittered and she
experienced a readiness to burst
with frustration at the night's
slow pace. When would the morrow
              come?

Chapter Seventeen

I needs must set things right. But first, Valerie needed to find a way to calm herself. *A cup of hot tea will soothe me.* She busied herself in her kitchen and when finished, sat with her hot drink in her rocking chair. When that didn't relax her, she moved to a wainscot chair beside the rocker.

Eventually, Valerie returned to her bed, but fidgeted until deep into the night. She couldn't relax no matter what she did. A full moon climbed to high into the night sky outside her bedroom window before she finally gave up her wakeful pursuit of rest and climbed from her bed.

She brewed herself more hot tea, and with cup in hand she returned to her rocker. All the

while she pondered over what the
next day's events would be. At
length, her eyelids grew heavy and
her ruminations ended. She
returned to bed, and managed to
nap before the sun rose with its
proclamation of a new day.

    The day's first rays of
promise peeked through her bedroom
window's wooden shutters when
Valerie woke.. She frowned when
she rose because she realized
she'd slept in her dress from the
day before. It bore the wrinkles
of her fitful night. She couldn't
believe her worry caused her such
forgetfulness' to change on the
night before.
    This will never do. She
needed to make a good presentation
in Smithton. *I needs must be busy
if I am to be dressed proper and
into Smithton at the proper hour
for this morning's town meeting.*
She rushed outside with worry
about her mode of dress put off
until later.
    She needed to harness and
hitch her horse to her wagon.
With the conveyance's brake on, it
would wait for her. On her way
back to her cottage, she rehearsed
the things she should say to the

114

magistrate and settlers of the township.

She counted each point on her fingers. *I be a natural healer. . .* Her thoughts turned to spoken words as she busied herself. "But I be not a witch." She shoved her fists down to her sides in fury with the implications.

"Wherefore can they not accept me as I am?" She took a moment and massaged the pain in her temples with her fingers. When Valerie reached her cottage, it came time she worried about the way she dressed.

Upon reaching the area she slept in, she frowned when she saw only one clean day dress hung in her free-standing closet. The dress, made from several food sacks sewn together, hung straight and lifeless on her.

'Twill not make such a good impression. She only wore the garment while she worked about her home. *'Tis not my favorite, but I suppose it needs must do.* After she dressed; Valerie paused and straightened to her full height. *I must be strong today. Wherefore should anyone care what I wear?*

Her nerves tingled in fear of what might happen to her as she neared Smithton. Her hands fought to draw on the reins and turn toward home. The nervous reaction of her body twisted her insides, but she swallowed hard and continued on her way.

On her entrance into Smithton, Valerie searched out the main street, but didn't see anyone. *The adults must already be at meeting. No changelings. They be all locked away,* she reminded herself. She breathed deep for confidence and reassurance. *At least I have put Scotty away in a protected place until my return.*

She stopped the wagon and tied her horse to a rail outside the meeting hall. Then she ran her hands down her sides to straighten her dress as best she could. She took one more deep breath and climbed up the two wooden steps to the establishment's door.

The meeting drew to an immediate and obvious abrupt halt when she opened the door and stepped inside. A haze of cigar smoke filled the air. Mugs remained raised, and jaws dropped.

Valerie nodded, smiled and slid into an empty seat.

"Ahem." The lead orator cleared his throat and called the meeting back to order, "Silence!" he called amidst the already ordered room. He cleared his throat again and continued. "We have a visitor today. Good morrow, Miss Valerie. It be most fitting ye have chosen this morrow, of all morrows, to join us for our assembly."

Valerie's face warmed.

"Sir?" she inquired.

"Ye be our topic on this morrow."

The warmth on her forehead moistened and she no longer noticed the pace of her heart. She feigned ignorance. "I am? What could thy concern on my account be?"

"As ye have probably noticed, by their lack of visits to ye, we have a problem with ye and our children."

She employed selective hearing in her reply, "But they are still brought to me if they have problems. I help them."

The magistrate cleared his throat and continued, "At this time we are here to discuss what appears to be a problem ye have *caused*, not helped with."

Valerie did notice when her pulse throbbed this time. The skin over her entire body moistened. *I must stay collected and protest my innocence.* With as even a tone as possible, she asked, "And the problem I have not helped with, is?"

The lead man jabbed an accusatory finger at her and raised his voice. "A few have claimed ye enchanted them! We understand ye be a witch!"

She stood up from her seat on shaky knees. Her lungs emptied of air, her face chilled, and her head lightened. *'Tis no time for this reaction.* The time had come for her to defend herself.

"But I have not. Verily; they lie!" she cried out in her own defense.

"Then explain wherefore they act the way they do after they see ye!"

Chapter Eighteen

Valerie cast her anxious vision about her. Her panicked focus swept the entire room. She swallowed hard and forced calm over herself when she at last spoke.

"I experience their emotions and ken they are lonely and bored. Some of the young ones here even feel ignored by the rest of ye. To me, it seems they only want some attention, and that is the reason they act out."

She looked at the disapproval in the faces aimed at her. It reminded her of reactions when Hendrick condemned her because of her barrenness. She continued, nonetheless, "I have done nothing evil."

Valerie flailed her hands out to her sides in an effort to make them listen to her. "I have glimpsed thy changeling's emotions. I allow them to understand their thoughts. I pray thee, believe me! It be not witchery I practice.

"Thy children grow stronger under my care and that must be wherefore they chose to show their exaggerated expressions to ye."

At the end of her monologue, Valerie offered her opened palms out to the room full of those who laid blame on her. "They love me for the good I have done them."

"If 'tis so, then wherefore do they now denounce ye?" the magistrate thundered.

She turned to the civil officer and her voice trembled in her response. "I ken not wherefore! It be a mystery to me as 'tis to ye. I pray thee; believe me. I have not harmed any of them!" She paused for a moment before she ventured to ask, "Have they saith I be a witch?"

An older male colonist in the magistrate's congregation stood and shouted through his long white beard at her. "No! 'Tis what *we* saith! Ye witched them! We ken that!"

"How do ye ken that?" Valerie asked with controlled respect for her elder.

"In any other case, "they would not act the way they do," he responded with certainty.

Valerie widened her eyes and stared at him through sudden tears. Her pulse pounded. Light-headedness from her sleepless night crept over her. The room swam. *I can bear no more—not today.* She lifted her skirt, turned, and marched from the building. *I will retain my dignity.*

"Ye take heed! We be watching ye!" the head magistrate shouted after her.

It was only as she left the room she noticed Alecksander sat in attendance. He raised an eyebrow at her as she departed. It appeared he took great interest in all that happened at the meeting.

Valerie knew she indeed exhibited great fortitude in the face of her accusers, and absolute innocence to any part in the trials the changelings exhibited. Her only hope lay in that he saw that, and thought her innocent.

Alecksander took Valerie by surprise when he again chose to ride to her home the next morning. She dropped a piece of laundry she intended to hang out to dry, and snatched it back up before it hit the ground. She held it up to her chest as a shield at his approach atop his shiny black Stallion.

"Wherefore be ye here?" she snapped at him when he pulled up on his horse and stood within earshot.

"I be here because ye told me I could call on ye."

Valerie released an audible huff. *He keeps falling back on that excuse.* "Do ye not recall that I rescinded that offer?"

He paused for just an instant, as if caught by surprise before he continued, "And I still wish to ken more about ye," he answered. He gazed about, like he expected to see someone else.

She eyed him with suspicion and kneaded the fabric she held at her breast. "And wherefore be it ye wish to ken more about me?"

Alecksander dismounted and left his compliant horse to stand. Valerie watched his every move and braced in defense as he neared her.

The slow, steady steps he took forward alarmed her. He appeared like a predator in stalk of its prey. Her abdomen tightened.

Valerie's firm hold on herself soon smoothed into an erotic tremble. She wished her body would not respond to his the way it did, but she couldn't help it. The excited physical sensations which wove through her body bade her to welcome him, but the strength of her instinct for self-survival warned she should once more send him away.

The man came right to the point when he stood within a couple arm's distance from her. "Ye be a beautiful young woman, and in case ye could not tell, I be both physically and emotionally attracted to ye."

Valerie's resistance softened even more at his seductive words. *Curses!* Like she could, or should care. *Mayhap he tricks me.* That thought squelched any further melt of her conflict with him.

Wherefore should I care he be 'attracted' to me? The man thinks too much of himself.

His proximity to her weakened her, in spite of her resolve. The fevered heat of a passion she never knew washed over her. His body attracted her while his self-assurance repelled her.

Valerie's fingers allowed the garment she held to fall back into its basket. She took a deep breath that bubbled around her heart as the organ pulsated. She could not find a word to say to him. Nor could she trust any words she might say to him.

He reached out and touched her cheek with a gentle finger. It slid down to and under the tip of her chin, where it remained. "I would like to believe ye have the same attraction to me," he uttered in a low provocative tone.

The mischievous sparkles in his eyes captivated and tickled her in the most intimate places. *Stay away from him!* Scotty's words would not leave her in peace. They served their purpose.

She jerked her face away from his hypnotic finger. *The gall!* "No. I do not have that 'same attraction' to ye," she lied. *The man touches me like we already ken intimacy between each other.*

"Then I suppose 'tis in vain I visit ye and 'twould be best I should leave," he calmly announced as if he had no further interest in the matter.

Valerie's heart fell into the basement of her soul at the way he dismissed her in such a casual manner. *He does not even look hurt at my rejection of him.* That thought alone plagued her about what might be. *Mayhap 'tis for the best.*

She managed one coherent comment she trusted, "Yes. I s'ppose ye should." His long lean legs hoisted him up onto his horse and he cantered the animal away without even another word between them.

****

That didn't go so well. 'Twas for the best.' Alecksander could not raise her suspicions about what his true motive might be in their future relationship. *And there* will *be a 'future relationship.'* Of that he remained certain. How should he proceed?

He cogitated over his dilemma as Penumbra carried him along the windswept trail that led into the Smithton Township. *A child will get me into her good graces. The boy be the key.* He decided his first move should be to develop

125

trust with Scotty. On that note,
he prodded Penumbra into a more
purposeful canter into Smithton.

Chapter Nineteen

Alecksander entered the village amidst a great disturbance. Colonists hustled along the packed earthen paths by the road. Excited voices assailed his ears. He pulled up on Penumbra when a turbulent commotion of colonists billowed from the town salon. Angry settlers soon surrounded him. The conglomeration of colonists shouted at him in a multitude of voices. "She be at it again! Wherefore have ye not done something about the witch?"

Alecksander cocked his head back in disdain at their tumultuous approach. Penumbra spooked and pranced in place under his tight rein. He raised a resolute hand into the air ahead of him and demanded of them, "Silence!"

The lead magistrate strode forward from the stunned crowd. "It still happens! Our children continue to come under the curse of the witch!" he exploded.

Shouts again arose from the agitated colonists crowded behind him.

"My baby be in fits!" a middle-aged woman cried out.

The magistrate turned toward her and shoved his flattened palm down toward the ground in an effort to shush her hysteria, and then turned back and glared at Alecksander. "What have ye learned about the woman we suspect?"

Alecksander kept his gaze into the magistrate's eyes and didn't blink. That he actually learned more about *his* own desires than about her, would not be a truth he told at this time. "Ye assume I have found Miss Valerie be a witch." He paused for effect before he continued, "That, I have not."

The crowd inhaled an audible intake of air.

Alecksander scanned them in a slow moment of study. "Rest

assured. I will find thy answer for ye, but 'twill take more time. I need to keep her under my observation and wait for her to give herself away to me."

At this, the agitated matron cried, "We have trusted her with our babies! Has she not already given 'herself away' by the way they now act?"

Alecksander focused on the woman, and willed her to silence. When he again spoke, it was for her ears only, "She has not already shown herself to *me*." To the crowd he explained, "*I* need to see her exposed before I turn her over to ye as a witch."

Alecksander then remained silent while he faced his inner turmoil. *I cannot charge Miss Valerie as a witch. I do not see evil in her. I experience connection in her and with her. But of that I must be sure.* His considerations pummeled his belief system as he left the meeting salon.

"Master Witch Hunter!" the magistrate called after him.

"I will soon have full control of the matter," Alecksander responded from outside the salon's front. Yes. Taking

Scotty with him to her cottage would accomplish his objective for him. *She will never turn the boy away.* He could control her very easily with the child in his hand. *I need ignore the magic she casts over me.*

Alecksander donned the same smug grin of success he did each time he brought a witch to justice. He rubbed his palms together and strode over to the building where the colonists kept the changelings.

The afflicted children all crowded around Alecksander with their crazy antics the instant he entered the quarantined building. Each again did his best to outperform the other with crazy behavior. He did a visual search over their heads with eyes for only one child. *Whence could that boy be?*

The generously proportioned matron from before rushed to his side, this time to shoo the rambunctious changelings away from *him*. She bowed her head and apologized for their actions, "I be sorry, Master Witch Hunter, they be uncontrollable in their tormented states of mind."

She formed a peak with her hands under her chin in a humbled position. "Do ye have more observations ye would like to make at this time, Mr. Witch Hunter?" The woman batted her eyes and preened at his presence.

"I have come to see the boy Scotty, again," he replied with no more of a glance than it took for him to note her flirtatious actions. "But I do not see him."

"Ah, sir! That boy keeps to himself. We often do not ken whence he be, ourselves."

Alecksander kept up his visual search through the building. He paid her continued self-conscious actions no mind.

"Ye may wander through this cottage and see whence he be found," she offered along with an outstretched sweep of her meaty arm over the action-packed room.

"Thank ye," he stated without another glance in her direction.

Alecksander didn't see Scotty anywhere. *I did not expect it be so hard to meet with the boy again. I must remedy that.* He then left the building of quarantine.

On his exit, Alecksander closed his eyes and steadied his

breathing in a moment of meditation. When he opened them again, he knew exactly where he should go. He and Penumbra were soon well on their way away from Smithton.

* * * *

Valerie's life returned to as normal as could be expected after the witch hunter's visit. After several days she managed to push him from her mind and resumed her counsels with changelings.

Although she sensed the distrust of her in their parents; her talent for empathy left her no peace from the care she gave to the young ones.

At her weakest moments, Valerie believed the clamor in her mind a curse. The turmoil she experienced amongst the changelings tormented her.

Even when she didn't spend her time in direct discussion with the young ones, Valerie absorbed the unrest of their emotions. She wished those of Smithton village proper hadn't stopped their regular visits with her.

I be glad Scotty be kept safe from this fervor with my native friends, and he be free to visit me again.   I wonder wherefore the settlers don't miss him?

She sent her gaze toward the township. *Why haven't they noticed he's not returned to the place they held him?   Do they not care about their afflicted charges?*

Chapter Twenty

Scotty saw the witch hunter when the man raced his horse into the Wampanoag village. Alecksander's quick approach and the blackness of his animal's color evoked a sense of dread in the boy.

He held his breath and watched as the unexpected visitor did a visual search throughout the village. The boy keenly observed the man's conversation as it ensued with the tribal Sachem.

His chest tightened and a lump rose in his throat. *I hope 'tis not for me he looks. 'Tis bad in him. He wants to hurt Miss Valerie.* His breath skipped in panic when the witch hunter ceased his conversation and looked toward him.

Terror froze his bones. The boy had assumed he couldn't be seen in his concealed spot, but knew the man saw him. *He doesn't like me either, because I love Miss Valerie.*

Scotty watched in wide-eyed alarm as the witch hunter paced through the camp and approached the location where he hid in an old white pine tree. Scotty's neglected lungs ached with every step the man took toward him.

The witch hunter soon reached and stood at the bottom of Scotty's supposed safe haven. Faintness from the length of time he held his breath begged to overtake Scotty.

It seemed to the boy that in an effort to hide him, the old pine's needled branches even ceased to wave in the breeze. *I thank ye ol' pine for thy protection.*

Alecksander looked up into the dark growth of the multiple branches. "Come down from there, Scotty. I wish to speak with ye again."

Scotty swallowed hard. His anxious heart beat against his chest in a flurried frenzy. *He be guessing. Verily he cannot hear*

my heartbeats. But how else could
he ken I'm up here in this old
tree?

"I ken," Alecksander said, as
if in reply to the boy's thoughts.
"Come down now. I want to talk to
ye."

Scotty tensed his little body
so hard it hurt, at Alecksander's
implied answer.

* * * *

No movement came from the
tree in response to Alecksander's
request. It became obvious, even
to the Great Witch Hunter, he
frightened the child.

Alecksander reprimanded
himself in silence. *'Tis not an*
adult ye speak to. Ye must speak
kinder.

"I pray thee, come down,
Scotty. I want to be ye friend.
I ken ye be up there. I ken ye
hear me. Won't ye come on down
from there and speak with me?"

Alecksander smiled when he
heard movement and saw a pair of
skinny little legs emerge from the
shadowy void of white pine
needles.

"Ah, there ye be, me lad!" he
exclaimed. "Here, allow me to
help ye down from there."

"I can do it, myself!" Scotty shouted and kicked when Alecksander attempted to help him.

Taken aback, Alecksander retreated with wounded arms. He rubbed them while he watched the accomplished little tree climber shimmy down by himself.

When his feet hit the ground, Scotty turned to face the witch hunter. His eyes narrowed. "'Tis ye want?"

Alecksander smiled. "I told ye, I would like to be ye friend."

The boy did not change the doubtful nature of his expression. "Wherefore?"

"Because I thought we developed an understanding the first time I visited that place whence they kept ye, and I took ye away from there for a visit with Miss Valerie."

Scotty stiffened his already obstinate pose and slid the toes of one of his unclad feet back and forth in front of him.

Alecksander imagined the line figuratively separated them.

The time does not exist for me to be involved in this.

Alecksander stared at the obstinate child in front of him.

Ye must listen to me.

Scotty's toes ceased their movement, but he didn't appear to listen.

At the illustrated lack of control he could place on the boy, Alecksander bit back his pride and kneeled in front of the child.

Scotty wouldn't even shift his gaze straight ahead into Alecksander's eyes.

"I ken ye must feel alone here with these people of a different civilization." When the boy still did not move, Alecksander asked, "I pray thee will let me be ye friend so ye will be no longer alone."

"Back at that place, I only used ye to get out to see . . . ." Scotty clipped his next words back as if he bit his tongue.

Alecksander sensed Scotty's reluctance to mention Valerie's name. On the other hand, he also remembered how the boy created his problem, by warning her against seeing him.

"And I did help ye get out and away from there. I could help ye again in other ways, as thy friend, if ye would allow me."

Scotty raised his face to Alecksander this time; his eyes narrowed even further. "Help me in what 'other ways'? I don't need to get out with ye again."

He waved his arm about in presentation of the Wampanoag village they stood in.

"These native people be my friends. Here, I can go to see Miss Valerie whenever I want to. I *saith* I only used ye before. Wherefore do ye want to be my friend?"

"I told ye," Alecksander responded with a slight harshness added to his voice. The Great Alecksander found himself very near the end of his kindness with this child.

I must control myself. 'Tis the key to any chance at a relationship with Miss Valerie I might have. That neither the boy nor the woman would submit to his influence churned his insides.

I must try again. He donned another smile, deceitful though it may be, and once more reached his hand out to Scotty. "Come now. Wherefore must ye suspect me of anything?

"What have I done to deserve that? I would say nothing. In order to be friends, we must first trust each other." *And then Miss Valerie will trust me.*

"No! I do not want to be thy friend!" Scotty emphasized with a stomp of his foot. "And I do not want Miss Valerie to be thy friend, either!"

The boy's deliberate response shook Alecksander. The man jerked back as if slapped. "Wherefore do ye say that?"

Scotty jabbed one of his skinny little fingers into Alecksander's face. "I ken ye be a witch hunter!"

Chapter Twenty-One

"And?" Alecksander asked in
quick response.
"And I ken they think Miss
Valerie a witch!"
"They do? May I ask who be
they?"
Scotty sent a hard glare at
Alecksander, as if he should know
who the boy spoke of. "Those ol'
grownups in Smithton."
Alecksander slipped his
thumbs into the side pockets of
his soft leather breeches at the
boy's blatant show of disrespect,
and settled in with a game of
questions. "Wherefore do ye think
that?"
The boy pointed outside the
native camp toward Smithton.
"Because of those coxcombish girls
who live there."

"Wherefore do ye refer to them as foolish?"

"They've acted out and blamed Miss Valerie for their actions. They made everyone think Miss Valerie be a witch."

Alecksander held his composure. "How does that involve me?"

Scotty poked his index finger straight up between them in emphasis. "I may not be ten years, yet, but I ken a lot more than ye think. Ye *ken* wherefore. Ye be a witch hunter and they want ye to hand her over to them."

"And so now ye won't go with me to only visit with her?"

Scotty stomped one of his feet. "No!"

Alecksander straightened with a show of nonchalance from his casual pose and pretended to turn and leave Scotty alone by the tree. "Then I guess I'll go to see her by myself."

"No! Ye can't!" the boy screamed.

Alecksander turned back and noticed Scotty driven to tears at this point in his energetic act of defiance. The witch hunter stopped and sighed at the fear he'd placed in the boy. "'Tis wrong now?"

"I l-love Miss Valerie," Scotty sobbed. "I do not want ye to hurt her."

"And what about those changelings? Do they not love Miss Valerie, too?"

Scotty dried his eyes with the backs of his hands. "Yes. We all love Miss Valerie, but they used her for an excuse to not get into trouble for bad things they did."

"Then wherefore don't ye tell that to the grownups of the township?"

"I've tried! The others of us who have visited with Miss Valerie have all tried, but they will not listen to us. They listen to those men who come on ships."

"What stories do *those men* tell?"

"They say there are bad people who live with us and do bad things to us with their magic. And they think Miss Valerie does bad magic, too."

Alecksander considered the boy's words for a minute. "And 'tis wherefore ye stopped talking to anyone there?"

"Yes."

"And not because of *magic* Miss Valerie does?"

"No. I mean, yes." He stomped his foot. "Stop tricking me."

Alecksander flashed a grin. *Caught.* "Tell me, what exactly did those girls do that would get them into such trouble they would blame someone who helps them?"

"They started throwing fits whenever somebody wanted them to do something. Those popinjays threw food around and made messes. And then they wouldn't clean after themselves.

"They made up words that no one else could understand and acted like Tom's o' Bedlam." He threw his hands out to his sides in a burst of renewed excitement. "They did those things even during *church* meetings!"

That would drive most right-minded settlers to think bewitchment. It does sound like 'tis bewitchment, even if I don't want to believe it. I ken these things before . . .

Alecksander's guts twisted at his assumption, but he mentioned it to Scotty, anyway, "It could be that Miss Valerie indeed be a witch. Have ye entertained that worrisome thought?"

Scotty's face glowed red and he stomped his foot. "*No*! She be not a witch and I will not go with ye to see her *again*!"

Alecksander repeated himself, "Then I will take *myself* to see her."

"Ye cannot go to see her."

"Wherefore not?"

"I warned her."

"Of what?"

Scotty's face reddened and he glared at Alecksander. "I told her who ye are and what ye want to do to her and I made her *promise* not to let ye see her again!"

This does not help. "What if I promised ye that I would never do anything to hurt her? What if I told ye I loved her, too?"

The boy sucked in a sharp breath as if in full attention at the words he heard. He widened his watery eyes and looked directly into Alecksander's face. "Ye do? How can ye love her? Ye do not even ken her."

Alecksander didn't know how to answer that question. "I don't ken wherefore. I just do. Inside it seems I search for her."

"I ken. Ye *search* for
witches."
Alecksander's eyes closed in
frustration. Instead of giving
echo to his current thoughts about
the boy, he changed the subject,
"I already ken she won't see me
now ye told her what ye have."
"How do ye *already* ken that?"
"She told me so."
Scotty beamed in self-
satisfaction at Alecksander's
affirmation.
"She trusts ye."
Scotty nodded his little head
hard in agreement with
Alecksander's words.
The witch hunter repeated, "I
will not hurt her." *Someone else
might, but I won't.* "Ye must
believe me. She be a special
person. I only want to ken more
about her."
"I already ken she be a
special person, but how do I ken I
can believe ye?"
*'Tis not going as expected.
Need for another change of subject
be at hand.* "Do ye like to
angle?" Alecksander asked.
Scotty responded with a nod
of his head. He appeared
suspicious.

146

"How about if we do some angling? There be a river near here, be there not?"

Scotty drawled out a word, which appeared guarded, "Y-e-s."

The boy sounded extremely hesitant, but Alecksander noticed the spark in his eyes at the mention of angling. He slanted his head in the direction of the stream. "Come on, now."

"I don't have the proper 'quipment to angle with," Scotty challenged.

Alecksander eyed the boy in acceptance of his dare. "I happen to have the equipment we need." The witch hunter closed his eyes for a minute.

When he reopened them, he reached into a large pocket in his cloak and pulled out a wooden spool with a metal ring attached to it. The apparatus fit perfectly onto his thumb.

"But I don't want to be punished by the magistrate for my 'exercise of idleness'!" Scotty proclaimed with great vehemence.

The child will not stop his test of me. Alecksander recalled the popular opinion the colonists held of angling. *Angling with a hook and line be an exercise in idleness, which deserves punishment.*

He knew the prevailing sentiment well. The 'vice' of angling came due to its association with the aristocracy the colonists fled from in England.

He smiled and assured Scotty, "Trust me. Ye punishment for 'idleness' will not happen. Ye be no longer amongst the colonists, and I be sure thy new native friends here angle, too."

Scotty beamed, then immediately frowned. "But we have no hook."

Chapter Twenty-Two

"I have already told ye, I have all we will need." Alecksander pulled a small hook from his pocket. It would be perfect for the small fish he knew swam in the nearby waters.

"'Tis too little," Scotty said.

"The fish that swim in the stream, which runs by Miss Valerie's cottage, be quite small, Scotty. I do not think they would be interested in a much larger hook."

The boy took a careful hold on the small hook Alecksander held out to him, and frowned. He looked at the hook as if he had no idea how it could be big enough.

Scotty then skewed his little face up toward Alecksander's. "Ye be sure 'tis big enough for those little fish in the stream to gorge themselves on?"

Alecksander gave him a confident nod.

"Be ye certain?" Scotty again asked.

"Yes, I be quite sure," Alecksander replied. "The one ye hold would do the job." He reclaimed the proffered hook from Scotty and attached it to the fine cord on his spool.

After he put it all back into the seemingly voluminous pockets of his cloak, he motioned to Scotty. "Come along, now," he invited. They left the Wampanoag village.

Soon they were seated on the bank of Miss Valerie's stream. Alecksander picked a quiet spot for them to angle together downstream from where his target lived.

The witch hunter softened his face, gave his angling partner a friendly expression and said, "Let us see if the fish be biting here today, shall we?"

He leaned back and prepared to launch the hooked twine into the water. Before he had a chance to cast it, Scotty threw himself toward him.

"Let me cast it! Let me! Oh, let me!"

Alecksander allowed his self-satisfaction to return. *My ruse be accomplished. The boy has forgotten our previous topic.*

The two spent many afternoons together angling downstream in the small river that ran alongside Miss Valerie's cottage. They continued their regular angling trips until the day Alecksander believed they'd grown to be great friends.

"Twould be a good time to talk to him about Miss Valerie again. The days grew shorter and he hoped to reacquaint himself with the woman before the winter storms set in.

"I bet Miss Valerie can cook these fish up better than I," he casually mentioned to Scotty one day, before their meal.

The boy immediately jumped up from where he sat, on an old log on the river's bank, with his line. "We should take the string of fish we caught today, to her."

A good sensation of gratification warmed Alecksander's insides. *Job done. He trusts me enough to take me to see Miss*

Valerie. We should go before he changes his mind.

"My stomach just growled. I think we should go to see Miss Valerie right away."

"Ok!" Scotty pulled his line in faster than Alecksander.

****

Horse hooves outside her small home brought Valerie's attention up from the garment she stitched. *Who be that?*

Unannounced visitors didn't often happen by her cottage, yet now they seemed to with regularity since the witch hunter arrived in Smithton.

Valerie stood and put down the day dress she worked on. She wandered to her door and peeked out its window.

A horse and rider approached her home through the trees. Her insides chilled when she recognized the horse's dark shade as it pranced closer, and wove back and forth between the trees.

She made out another, much smaller rider behind the first. She balanced on her tiptoes and peered out the small high sun-window on her door as best she could, to determine if she recognized the second rider.

"'Tis Scotty!" *Scotty? Wherefore be he with that witch hunter?* Of even more importance, she believed nobody, besides the native folk, knew where she'd placed the boy.

The reason behind that fact, or who brought him to her at this time, lost its immediate importance. She needed first to ensure his safety.

Valerie jerked her front door open and ran out into her front yard to greet them. "Scotty! Be ye all right?"

Scotty's sheepish little face peeked out at her from behind Alecksander's much larger form. "Holla, Miss Valerie."

He scrambled down from behind Alecksander before the horse appeared to possess even the slightest inclination to stop. The boy's little feet moved before he hit the ground.

The two dear friends met each other halfway in the short distance between them. A flurry of emotion followed while they hugged each other.

Then Valerie remembered who again brought her favorite little boy to see her. She sent a suspicious glare at the man, and then looked to Scotty. "How did he find ye?

Scotty shook his head so hard it looked like it would come off. His locks fell across his eyes as they so often did. His tongue stumbled over itself in answer.

"I pray thee believe me. I don't ken." Then his eyes widened as if in sudden realization and he tumbled into apology, "I be sorry I brought him here again."

Valerie skewed her eyebrows in question. Then she darted her eyes to Alecksander and back to Scotty. "But I thought..."

"Me too," Scotty answered. "But he says he wants to be our friend!" Then the boy changed the subject, "We have some fish that needs must be cooked."

Valerie breathed a brief chuckle at the short attention span of the boy whom she loved so much. She turned toward the man in question and greeted him with a small nod of her head, "Good morrow, sir."

Alecksander cocked his head to one side at her cold greeting. *Sir?* "I thought we might renew our acquaintance on a more familiar basis, but ye remain distant when ye call me, 'sir.'"

In an air of disdain for his error in belief, Valerie tilted her head slightly to her side and lifted her nose into the air.

"From all I hear of ye, I prefer not to be familiar in our acquaintance. But pray thee; do tell how ye came by my young companion here."

Scotty fidgeted by Valerie's side with the string of fish he held. They glistened as if fresh from the water. She couldn't imagine how he managed to dismount and rush to her side without harm to them.

"Wherefore don't ye go clean those fish and I'll cook them up for thy dinner," she suggested to quiet the boy's anxiety. His absence would also allow her to speak with Alecksander in private.

Scotty looked up at her. His attention switched back and forth between her and Alecksander.

Chapter Twenty-Three

Torn by Scotty's indecisiveness, Valerie knew she needed to set him at ease. "'Tis good," she assured him, then waved her hands away from them. "Now get on with ye."

Scotty's face lit up and he hoisted his catch to a shoulder. He quickly skipped off to the bubbling stream behind her cottage.

Valerie stared after the excited child and ignored the man's presence until proper etiquette awakened her to a sense of her blatant rudeness.

He may not be my choice of visitor for the day, but he be here and I should extend some sort of welcome to him.

She shifted her attention from the direction Scotty took.

"I pray thee, excuse my inhospitality. I be so happy to see Scotty again. The boy be my favorite of the village children."

Her gaze to Alecksander turned curious. "That be my reason for wondering how ye ken where I put him. I thought the Wampanoag camp be a safe place."

The witch hunter's expression never changed to one she could read.

"I did not ken whence he be. The natives here are friends of mine, too." A quick twitch of his lip alerted her to weigh his words for their truthfulness while she listened further.

"I came upon him at a time whilst I shared a meal with them. I be sure ye see him a lot there, too, but I have never seen ye there."

Her suspicion rose with his last words. "Ye have *never seen* me there? Does that mean ye have seen him there more than one time?" She glanced in the direction Scotty took. *He has not mentioned that to me.*

Something even more curious flashed across he man's expression when she returned her gaze to him. *I might tell something by that.*

Does he wait *for me to say something harmful about myself?*

I shall turn this back to him. "'Tis not about me, 'tis about ye."

His face remained straight, as if he thought of nothing, when he answered. "Yes. I have visited him there on more than one occasion.

He motioned between the native camp and her home. "We've also angled together in thy stream at a place between here and there, at times."

"'Tis told by the Wampanoag ye also visit with Scotty in their camp on occasion. There be the reason I noticed I've not seen ye in their village. Do ye not go there any longer?"

"*Yes* I do, though not as much as he comes here to see me." Her face warmed with her thoughts of the boy. "But 'tis not the case," she reminded him. "Wherefore be ye interested in him?"

"He be a lonely child."

Even with the compassion in his answer, Valerie still distrusted him. She didn't take a witch hunter as one who would be interested in the emotional welfare of others.

He tricked Scotty in some way. And now he tries to trick me. "'Tis an orphan," she offered in explanation of Scotty's plight. She placed her palms on her breast.

"I believe he and I belong together." Her hands removed from her chest and cupped together in front of her as she bade Alecksander good-bye, "I thank ye for bringing him to me today."

Alecksander spoke up as she turned to leave him. "I, too, have concluded the boy 'tis the reason for my visit to this settlement."

Valerie turned back to him and lowered her eyelids askance in question of his statement. *What lie be this?* She watched as he took what appeared to be a measured step toward her.

Her insides tightened and she immediately moved back an equal number of paces away from him. He spoke to her as he approached, "Please don't fear me."

The strong and smooth timbre of his words intoxicated her senses. *'Tis as if he means to coax me somewhere I do not wish to be.*

He stopped his advance at her retreat. "I pray thee, Miss Valerie, I mean ye no harm." His next words came to her in a halted fashion, as if they were hard for him admit.

"What I do mean . . . 'tis I feel a connection to the boy, and to ye, too." His hands entered, and then left the side pockets on his cloak. "Tis not something I ken well."

His vulnerable voice soothed Valerie's soul, but still she fought it. *Yet somehow I ken that I be meant to experience this.* The familiarity between them puzzled her.

Her emotions begged her to trust him and to welcome him into her life as she now knew it. But she refused her inner urging. *I do not ken this man. I do not want to ken this man. He be a witch hunter.*

She seized the moment and voiced her suspicions with vehemence, "How do I ken that? 'Tis not what I hear about ye, or ye intentions."

"And 'tis ye hear?" he asked. He stood his ground in the length that still separated them.

"I hear there be villagers in Smithton who suspect me of witchcraft."

His up-to-now authoritative expression turned unpretentious. "And 'twould that have to do with me?"

Valerie stiffened her back into a strong and straight posture and wagged a finger at him. "I pray thee, do not take me to be an idiot," she retorted with quick sarcasm.

He cocked his head at her remark. The return of his smug attitude ground her insides.

"I ken ye be a witch hunter," she accused.

He didn't deny a thing, just did a quick sweep of the ground with his vision before he rested it on her again. "That be not wherefore I be here."

Valerie would not be played by him. She tossed her head back and readied for her charge. "Oh? Be it not true that those same settlers have asked ye to give me to them as a witch, and 'tis verily the reason ye be here?"

He hung his head in a slight tilt with a setback mannerism she'd not yet seen. It bolstered her confidence. *I have effect on him.* After a deep breath, he confessed, "Yes. They did ask me to do that."

After his admittance, Alecksander raised his countenance to her again and she sensed he reasoned with her, "But again I tell ye their request be not the true reason I be here."

She cast an askance glance at him from the imagined high place where she looked down on him. "But ye did agree to do their bidding, did ye not?

"And verily, be that not how ye make thy way in this world?" He took another deep inhalation. *He will need to think long and hard on his response to that question.*

This time when Alecksander responded, he did so without his downcast appearance, but looked her straight in the eye. His strong and silent gaze sent chills through her. "Yes I did, and yes I do, but again I tell ye

"'tis not for that reason I choose to see ye. Ye must believe me. I saith to ye, 'tis hard for me to describe, but I sense 'tis a connection exists between us. Do ye not sense it, too?"

Chapter Twenty-Four

Valerie needed to make her own calculated response. *Yes, I do discern the link between us.*

Her hormones and all the intimate places in her experienced the connection he spoke of. *I cannot let my guard down.*

"I be quite sure I do not ken what 'connection' ye speak of," she answered with her best high and mighty expression.

Valerie assured herself Alecksander would never know whether she spoke the truth, or not.

Scotty rounded the corner of the cottage at a jog. He balanced a trencher of fish, with precarious precision. Alecksander had no opportunity to give his response to her.

"I got the fish unsullied and ready for ye to cook now, Miss Valerie!"

She accepted the dish of fresh fish from him when the boy reached her side. But she didn't take them straight to her kitchen. Instead, she turned the meats in a visual inspection of their readiness for her to cook.

Scotty's impatience skewed his face at her obvious insinuation she didn't trust his job. "I cleaned them real good and even went into thy kitchen and got that clean plate to put them on!"

"I can see that!" Valerie exclaimed as she continued her perusal of the dish filled with the three whole, headless fish.

Allow me to build thy fire," Alecksander offered. Without a word of approval from Valerie, he gathered kindling from the ground and carried it to a cooking pit dug just outside her cottage.

"That would be good of ye," Valerie responded. "Make sure 'tis built well and not too small. It shouldn't take long for us to roast these over a suitable fire."

After she issued her instructions, Valerie hurried over to her garden. She returned with

several ears of corn bundled into
her folded arms. "We should roast
these on the fire along with the
fish."

It didn't take long for
Alecksander to have the 'good
fire' built. "Allow me." He took
the fish from Valerie and ran the
fire place's spit through them.
Then he slowly turned them over
the small inferno.

Valerie could not help but
appreciate the man, despicable as
he might be, took on both the
fire's creation and the task of
turning the meat on the spit.

It would take but a short
time for their meal to cook, but
she rubbed her upper arms in
sympathy, anyway. They ached as
she recalled all the hours spent
while she prepared meals on the
spit by herself, switching arms as
required.

In the best spirits of her
day, she returned to her kitchen
for some dinner dishes. When she
re-emerged from inside her
cottage, the sight before Valerie
sent the discomfort of déjà vu
through her.

Her stomach grew queasy at
the comfortable familiarity of her
surroundings. *They should not be*

this way to me. Of course I be
familiar with my own home, but
'tis different.
It seems so natural. Like
'tis so right we all be here
together in this small family
group. 'Tis like we always belong
together. She blinked back sudden
tears. The dishes she carried
clattered in her hands.

Alecksander looked up to
Valerie from the fire, before her
tremble ceased. "Be ye all
right?"

"Yes, it all be . . . I be
all right." She stumbled over her
tongue and stopped the word 'too'
before it escaped her mouth.
"Everything be all right," she
finished.

A breeze passed. It cooled
and reminded her of the warmth her
face held in the heat of her
unexpected experience. She
fumbled with the dishes in her
hands and readied the outdoor
bench table for their meal.

Scotty seated himself in
front of his food as soon as it
arrived. He also started right
into conversation with his angling
partner.

"These fish be good," he remarked through a mouthful of the meal.

Alecksander smiled and nodded to the boy. "Yes it be." Then he winked at Valerie, "'Tis a good idea we bring them to Miss Valerie for our mid-day serving of food."

Valerie's insides waved at his wink, but she said not a word.

Much to her delight, Scotty's animated speech continued and kept Alecksander occupied during the time they enjoyed their meal. Even so, she sensed Alecksander's constant perusal. *What does he watch for?*

At last she could take no more. Her palms landed firmly on the rough-hewn table in front of her. It and all on it reverberated from her swift action.

She captured both their attentions with the execution of her emotion, after which she rose and looked down on the witch hunter. He stared back up at her.

"Wherefore do ye keep thy attention on me?" she demanded.

"Wherefore should I not?" he asked at the same moment as Scotty exclaimed with his own answer to her question, "Because he thinks ye be a witch!

"He tricked me into bringing him here again today." As if in a final effort to show his sincere concern, Scotty added, "I tried to keep his interest away from ye."

Valerie watched as Alecksander gave the boy a calm eye. It peaked her suspicion.

Scotty played with his food and ignored Alecksander. His reaction gratified her.

Valerie continued her special attention to the two, but said nothing. *'Tis like he uses mind control.*

"I did no such thing," Alecksander said to the boy. And then he looked back up to Valerie, his expression less intense. "We caught some fish and agreed we should bring them here for ye to cook."

"Then wherefore did *ye* insist on cooking them?" Valerie demanded of Alecksander. She narrowed her eyes and asked in as low and diabolical a tone as she could, "Did ye think I'd put a curse on them?"

She flashed him a wicked grin and then took a pot of water she earlier set to boil over the fire,

to inside her kitchen. Within a
moment she came back out and
gathered the dishes to wash.

As surely as she felt the
cloth of her dress on her back,
Valerie sensed Alecksander
considered her as she walked away.
*I be sure by now he kens I do not
trust him. Whence does that leave
him and his profession?*

Valerie listened as she left.
Then she watched from her kitchen
window when he turned his full
attention onto Scotty.

★★★★

"Wherefore do ye tell her
such things?" Alecksander
questioned the boy. "I thought we
be friends, and ye ken 'tis not
true she should be afraid of me."

Scotty scooted over on the
bench seat, away from Alecksander.
"Our angling together be fun, but
I ken now I should not have come
here with ye today."

He narrowed his eyes. "Ye
did trick me. I do not *ken* ye do
not think her a witch. We be not
real friends. I heard the
magistrate tell ye to watch her,
and 'tis not that what ye do just
now?"

"I tell ye, 'tis not my true
reason to keep my eyes on her. I

have no motives other than I like
the sight of her and I want to
learn more about her for my own
pleasure, not for the magistrate's
or for anyone else's."
Scotty eyeballed him and
asserted in a very low tone, for a
child, "Ye still tricked me into
bringing ye here."

Chapter Twenty-Five

Alecksander tightened his lips and glanced in the direction Valerie took. He caught her when she ducked away inside her home. *She hides from me.*

He continued his conversation with Scotty while in the process of averting his attention from the cottage window. "Mayhap 'tis the truth of the matter," he mumbled.

When his focus returned to Scotty; he filled it with intent. "Ye be right. 'Tis the reason I 'tricked' ye. I want to be near to her." *I sense she belongs with me.*

He playfully jabbed at Scotty's shoulder. "Ye protect Miss Valerie too well. She wouldn't have allowed my visit unless I had ye with me. So in a way ye be right, but I'd prefer to

say I *convinced* ye to come here
with me."

Scotty opened his mouth as if
he made motion to argue the point.

Alecksander cut him off with
a finger held up in front of his
face. *There be no more of that.*
"I still tell ye; she holds my
attention because I would like to
ken her better for my own personal
reasons."

Scotty offered no argument.

****

Valerie overheard
Alecksander's last remark as she
stood at her back door. Reason
told her it would be a good time
to prepare for departure from her
home, but she needed to hear more.

She imagined the turmoil
inside his thought processes,
which no doubt matched her own.
Her keen sense of hearing served
her well in their conversation.

"Do ye think she be a witch?"
the boy eventually asked the witch
hunter in a not so sure tone of
voice.

Alecksander sat in silence.
"That I do not ken." The sound of
his voice also seemed more
contemplative to Valerie.

"Do ye want to ken?" Scotty asked. His tone of voice sounded agitated now.

Once more, the witch hunter paused. The forcefulness of his earlier expression returned when at length he stared straight into the boy's eyes.

In an ominous tone he reminded the child, "I be a Witch Hunter. It matters not what I want to ken. If she be a witch, I will ken."

Scotty and Valerie both squirmed. Her palms moistened. Her stomach turned. She could listen no more.

****

Scotty continued his mission out of Valerie's earshot. "Ye say thy job be not the reason ye want to ken her better. If 'tis true, will ye make an oath to me ye won't turn her over to those in Smithton for something I ken be not true?"

Valerie convinced herself she should listen more and moved back to her earlier position.

"Yes. That I do, Scotty."

'that I do," what? What have they agreed upon?

Scotty confronted him. "Ye have lied to me afore now."

The boy's heated response told Valerie all she needed to know about the truthfulness of Alecksander's expression over whatever they discussed.

The witch hunter gave every impression he wouldn't be cowed by the boy with his response. "I tell ye the truth. If she be turned over as a witch, 'twill not be I who does it."

Something awful pressed against Valerie's insides. The sensation sent tingles of fright worse than ever before through her chest.

Alecksander's response confused her even more about his type of man or where his loyalties lay. The hardened pit of her stomach told her she couldn't trust him in her favor.

The queasy sensation of 'foreknowledge' beset her again. She watched in silence as the man and the boy continued in their serious conversation.

She trembled at their words. In an effort to quiet herself, she once more left her position and returned to her kitchen. *Mayhap 'tis best I give attention to the dishes and not to them.*

Valerie left the last dishes to soak in the water. Then she picked up a clean towel from a pine plank table nearby and dried her hands.

She appreciated the sight of them as they sat together beside the fire. They seemed so deep in solemn discussion with one another. *Like lord and son.*

When they stood and offered each other a firm handshake, she knew their conversation ended and the time came she could re-join them.

It wouldn't be good etiquette for her to return too soon and disturb an involved conversation between two such serious men.

She glanced up at the sun. It sat low on the horizon. Her gaze then set upon Scotty. "I do hope ye won't be leaving soon after we have supped."

Scotty looked up into her eyes. Then he sent a harder stare at the man who sat beside him. Butterflies flitted through her chest at his sudden lack of camaraderie with the man. *What have I missed?*

It appeared the witch hunter
paid Scotty, and his intense
scrutiny, little mind. Instead,
he set his dark eyes upon Valerie
in such a way she felt disrobed.
        "I think 'twould be good for
us to stay and share thy company
for a whilst," he said. A smile
lit up Scotty's face. It told her
of his interest to stay by her
                side, also.
        Her moment of reprieve from
the insinuation of Alecksander's
gaze, by Scotty's expressive
interjection, vanished at the
immediate predatory sparkle the
witch hunter's eyes showcased.
        The hairs on the back of
Valerie's neck tingled and danced
with apprehension. She regretted
her previous words of invitation.
        *He wants me to incriminate
myself. Mayhap I shouldn't have
issued an invitation to stay, or
at least in a way so as not to
                include him.*
        The witch hunter slid his
vision to the bench aside from
where he and Scotty sat. "Come.
I would like to ken more about ye.
Sit with us awhile and visit. Ye
fret too much over thy household
                duties."

*It be not about the household
duties I fret.*

"Yes. Come and sit here,"
Scotty agreed. He patted the seat
beside him. His hair bounced over
his face with unbounded energy.

Valerie's reserve softened at
Scotty's encouragement and she
took in the proximity of her
suggested place to sit. It
occupied the space next to the
witch hunter's. Her instincts
fought her not to approach it.

"Come now," Alecksander
invited along with a cast of his
head toward the empty area. "I
pray ye would not be so nervous
around me. I will not hurt ye. I
would only like to ken ye better,
that be all."

She didn't move. Even from
what she'd overheard, Valerie
still couldn't be certain of his
word. The cloth she held gave
under the anxious movements of her
fingers. After Scotty's repeated
urges, she overruled her instinct
and sat with them.

"I told him ye be a good
person and my best friend in the
whole world. Ye can believe him."
He flashed a quick, but serious
eye toward Alecksander. "He gives
his word he won't hurt ye," Scotty

assured her in all sincerity. "Ye can talk to him."

Valerie smiled at the boy's words. Her heart slowed and her moist skin cooled. The boy had an above average intelligence and intuitive ability. She believed she could trust in his word.

Chapter Twenty-Six

Mayhap he does not think me a witch. We shall see. "And I would like to ken more about ye, *too,*" she admitted in slow reluctance to Alecksander.

He folded his palms on his lap and settled in as if ready for an honest exchange. "Ye begin," he told her.

I needs must be careful with my words. Mayhap 'tis best if we talk about him. "Ye be a witch hunter. 'Tis a peculiar profession." She placed a hand on her breast.

"I don't believe in such doers of evil, myself. I pray thee, ye first tell me about ye and wherefore ye have chosen to hunt those creatures, if they do exist?"

179

He placed one of his hands to his chin and massaged it. "They do exist," he assured her with a solemn voice. "'Tis not a job I have chosen without much thought."

She observed an intense glow of knowledge in his eyes. It sent uneasy tension through her chest. *It be as if he searches into my soul.*

"Oh?" she queried in an uncomfortable breath.

He slid his vision away from her. The smooth way he spoke in quick accordance with her thoughts set her more at ease.

"Like ye, I have my doubts as to the amount of evil magical practitioners be about, or even if they exist here in Smithton.

"Given my personal knowledge of the ways of magic, I find witch hunting to be something I be well suited for."

"Oh?" she reiterated.

When he looked at her again, it seemed his visual interrogation of her began anew. "I be drawn to places whence anomalies like witches exist."

Valerie quietly asked, with hesitance, "Be ye drawn here?" *Does he hunt for me?* She rubbed her sweaty palms together. *When did they become moist?*

"Yes, I be drawn here."

The day's temperature grew uncomfortably hot for Valerie, as though she sat in a brick oven. She wiped her brow. Her clothes stuck to her body. She became a damp bundle of nerves.

His stern gaze never left her. "I speak the truth. I don't ken what 'tis ye do. I don't want to believe 'tis witchery, as the people of Smithton do, but 'tis ye and what ye do lured me here."

Butterflies in Valerie's chest went wild. *My dear sweet Lord! What did he mean by that? The man speaks in puzzles. He 'kens not' what 'tis I do, yet says he is 'drawn to places whence witches exist.'*

And he is . . . drawn here. Her last thought sickened her. A knot in her stomach weighed heavy. Her heart went into a frantic beat. *'Tis because he thinks I do witchcraft?*

Valerie hoped he didn't notice the strain in her voice when she forced her next question out, "What do ye mean by saying 'what I do'?"

She dizzied with the increased heart rate of her automatic defence, "I do not *do* anything. I be a caretaker for children, that be all."

He raised to her what appeared to be a quizzical eyebrow.   "The reason my services be called upon 'tis the *way* ye take care of them."

Valerie flinched at his tone of voice. *Best to be honest with him.* She folded her palms. "The 'way' I 'take care of them'? I pray thee, believe me. I only do what comes natural to me."

She paused and rethought her wording. "By that I mean I counsel by way of my intuition." She swallowed. *I be digging my hole deeper with every word I saith.*

She placed a hand on her chest in an act of innocence and digressed, "I love children. I be called upon to console and comfort them in my way when they experience difficult emotional problems. That be how I 'take care of them'."

He quirked an eyebrow at her. "Aye, thy 'way'. 'Tis told how ye connect to the young ones through ye *mind*. Be that the 'way' ye 'console and comfort them?"

Valerie scrunched her shoulders and took a deep breath. She pulled herself together as best she could while his dark gaze probed into her innermost being.

It sounded as if he believed his words when he continued his condemnation of her, "Tis also told ye exert control over them and ye change them in much the same way a witch would with her spells."

Her breath held. She widened her eyes and quick words of self-defence flowed out with her released breath, "No, that be not the way I help them."

The already extreme heat intensified in Valerie's world. Her heart pounded. She sought to avert her gaze, but Alecksander's magnetic vision held her entrapped. 'Tis a gift," she murmured.

"A 'gift'?" he mimicked.

Her hands massaged each other. "'Tis a special way I have with others—especially children."

He stared at her with anything but understanding of her words. "Be that not what a witch would have me believe?"

She raised her wide eyes back
up to him with newfound strength
and belief in herself, "I wouldn't
have ye *believe anything* a 'witch'
would. I'd have ye believe the
truth. I be not a witch; my ways
verily be a gift."
"Tis a 'gift' ye be born
with?"
"No. I awakened to my
connective abilities with others
whilst on-board the ship from the
old land to the new. They came
upon me whilst I cared for the
sick on the ship.
"From that time on I be able
to experience the troubles others
suffer in their minds. I be able
to join with and help them in
difficult times by use of my
mind's direction with them."
"And change them to thy
will?"
*He bends my words to say as
he would want.* "No. I don't
change them to my will. I counsel
and console them through their
troubles and help them to heal
themselves.
"The pitiable changelings
here need me and my
understanding." She stood with
her arms outstretched toward him

in an effort to make him
understand her urgency.

"Do ye not see? These
colonial changelings desire a
difference. They conjure a frenzy
to free themselves from the
stresses of life in this strange
new world."

His eyebrow rose again.
"'Tis an uncommon philosophy."

Valerie pressed her palms
together in front of her chin.
Her fingertips pressed onto her
lips while she spoke through them,
"Yes, I ken. 'Tis just a thought
I have."

"Be ye aware there be,
amongst the changelings in
Smithton, a few who accuse ye of
using, um, undue influence on
them?" His accusatory expression
remained unchanged.

Scotty, forgotten until this
time in the conversation,
disturbed them when he jumped to
his feet. "Those dumb ol' girls
just make up stories. Miss
Valerie doesn't make us do as she
wants.

"They blamed Miss Valerie so
they wouldn't get into trouble."
He ran to Valerie's side and threw
his arms around her. "Miss

Valerie be nice. She be not a witch."

Valerie's eyes misted as she looked down upon the child she loved so much. Then she raised her dampened vision to Alecksander again. "He be right. I be not a witch."

Her throat clenched at Alecksander's implied disbelief when he cocked his head in continued question. *I must make him believe me.*

She dried her eyes with her kerchief and sent him a pointed glare. "Those be not my words. They be the boy's own honest words and true opinion."

Chapter Twenty-Seven

"I would prefer to think ye not."

Valerie's tension eased at Alecksander's response. His crooked smile melted her insides. Suddenly she chilled and trembled with the change in her internal temperature.

"Ye be getting cold. Should we go inside?" Alecksander asked.

For lack of a better response, Valerie nodded. "Yes. The day passes quickly." She turned for her cottage and Alecksander and Scotty followed.

On second thought; she turned and held a hand before her, palm out, when she reached her door. "As I saith, the day passes' fast. 'Tis getting late. I believe ye should go now," she pointedly told Alecksander.

"If that be what ye have decided, then we shall go," Alecksander said. He motioned with his head to the boy beside him. "Come along, Scotty."

"No. I mean, *ye* may go, but leave Scotty with me," Valerie countered.

"If 'tis thy wish."

"Yes, 'tis my wish." *The time has come for me to take action and prove them all wrong. Scotty can help me with preparation tonight.*

Scotty scooted from under Alecksander's hand, and settled in close to Valerie's side. "Yes, I needs must do that."

Alecksander exhaled a deep breath. "I see. Then I will leave ye both." He turned and whistled. Penumbra trotted around Valerie's cottage and to his side. He left before Valerie said another word.

His prompt agreement to leave startled Valerie again. *No argument? I thought he wanted to ken me better. It should make me happy that he left so soon, but I am not.*

"Do ye still think he believes I be a witch?" she asked

Scotty while she watched the witch hunter ride away.

"I do not ken."

"Do ye think he will name me a witch if he thinks I be one?"

"No."

Scotty's immediate and decisive answer puzzled Valerie. She looked down to the boy. "How can ye be so sure?"

"I just be."

A breeze as chilled as her heart nuzzled through Valerie's hair. She wrapped her arms about herself and shivered, "Ooh. Let us go inside and find some blankets to bundle up in."

****

Alecksander pulled up on his mount when he topped a nearby ridge, his last chance to look back on Valerie's cottage. *I cannot think of her as a witch.* Penumbra snorted and shook his head as if in defiance.

The animal's decisive action reminded Alecksander of his negligence to his job. He shook his head at himself and what he had to do. *She has put a spell on me. That can only mean one thing.*

Alecksander knew he had a job to do. A job he had been hired for. He gave slack to the reins and Penumbra took him toward Smithton.

"He comes!" a male voice shouted when Alecksander rode onto the village's main street.

The witch hunter's attention perked up. He scanned the settlement. The man in question darted back into the meeting salon the minute the announcement escaped his mouth.

Alecksander continued on to the township's center building, dismounted and tied his horse. But he moved no further. The still air closed him in, like four walls.

An invisible partition encircled and held Alecksander in place. His breath faltered. He'd never encountered such a thing before. *'Tis not common magic.*

Alecksander released a breath he didn't realize he held when the same colonist re-emerged from the hall. The barrier of malevolence dissipated at the man's appearance.

"What be here?" Alecksander asked.

"Another witch hunter be here! He comes to us straight from the Old World. He be a

190

mighty one who hails from the ancient kingdoms in Europe."

"Wherefore be he here?"

"Ye have taken too long with thy assigned task. Mayhap this new witch hunter be even more powerful than ye!" the settler blurted in one long breath.

Alecksander jerked his head back in indignation at the colonist's remark.

The council member directed the witch hunter's attention back to inside the building. "He be inside right now!"

The reason, behind the illusion Alecksander encountered on his arrival, made itself known to him. "I didn't ken another be about. He comes from whence in Europe?"

"He saith not. He only saith he comes to do business here."

Alecksander stared into the abyss inside the shadowed hall's doorway. *The other has business here?* He tossed his long black cloak's tail out of his way.

It trailed behind him when he stepped onto the first step into the building. "Only one should be here. I will see to what business brings the man here."

The colonists inside stepped to one side in unison. An excited babble arose from the clustered together group as the witch hunter entered the building.

Alecksander imagined they expected to see a direct confrontation of wills between him and the other.

Chapter Twenty-Eight

A grizzled old man sat on a high slatted- back chair in the middle of the room. His left hand held onto the top-end of a gnarled cane. Its other end rested on the floor at his side.

The being's long tousled grey hair possessed a greenish sheen. Its aura arced out around him. His dark cloak glittered in defiance.

He glared at Alecksander. Alecksander stared back.

"Call me M."

A memory niggled in the back of Alecksander's brain as he returned with his own name. *I ken him, but from whence?*

The two men faced each other in formidable silence. Not a breath could be heard from their audience.

"Ha, Ha, Ha, Ha," M cackled.
He stood and held an arm out to
Alecksander. "Come, I have not
met another such as I in a very
long time. Welcome into my
presence."

Welcome into my *presence?*
Alecksander loosened his stance
and took a step toward M. "I,
too, have not met another such as
I in a long time."

*Never here in the New World,
that is.* He stayed his footsteps
and stated, "*Ye* are welcomed into
my presence." Each then advanced
on the other at the same slow
pace.

A collective gasp filled the
area when they met in the middle
and each threw out an arm toward
the other in what appeared menace.
The room sizzled in the tension
they created.

Human utterances and motion
once more filled the room at the
end of their perceived act of
threat. Wooden chair legs slid on
the floor as everyone returned to
their respective seats.

"From whence have ye come?"
Alecksander demanded of his rival.
And for what reason?" He
dismissed his foreknowledge and

therefore experienced no familiarity with the other.

When M answered, a spark Alecksander knew only he saw, leapt from the shadowed eyes of his supposed opponent. He could have caught the evil ember himself, if so inclined.

"I hear 'tis talk of witchcraft in this New World. 'Tis what draws me to sail across the seas from deep within the old land."

Both his questions answered, but not quite, Alecksander composed another question, "From how 'deep' in the old world do ye come?"

"From whence Jupiter rules, do I come."

Alecksander furrowed his eyebrows in thought. *Jupiter?*

Without a word, M answered Alecksander's unspoken curiosity in an instant. *Yes. Rome be my ancient homeland.*

His immediate answer enlightened Alecksander. *Ye share the thoughts of others.*

M nodded in concurrence.

That makes it so. We are both accomplished practitioners of the craft. And true adversaries if there be a witch to be hunted here.

M moved his head in the affirmative. His solemn expression warned the witch hunter he should take care.

Alecksander immediately closed his mind as thoughts of the suspected woman, whom so recently caught his amorous attentions, flowed through it.

No. I do not wish to bring more turmoil into her life. She 'be not a practitioner of the craft.

He couldn't implicate Valerie to this man. *M must not ken those thoughts.* "I have come to this place for the same reason as ye.

"After some investigation, and at much length, I be not too certain that one of the true practice, or a false practitioner, be here."

"I see," M said. "But ye have closed thy thoughts to me. Wherefore be that?"

The suspicion he heard in M's voice didn't bother Alecksander. "Privacy. Do ye not do the same, at times?"

M smirked. "I will do my own investigation."

Alecksander knew he'd encountered an evil man. *Valerie must be cleared of all suspicion in his eyes, be she guilty or be she not. I cannot allow her to fall into this man's hands.*

Yet, Alecksander knew he couldn't be the one to do it. *It might be to my peril. She holds too much power over me. I can't stay here any longer.*

I don't need a woman in my life. He reconsidered his position and decided to do nothing. *'Twill be as fate allows. If Valerie be found a witch, 'twill not be of my doing.*

Alecksander anticipated the impossibility of anyone finding her a witch. He imagined perhaps he should stand by and let M take over.

If the woman indeed be innocent, then regardless of his character, M will ken and testify before the magistrate to Valerie's innocence.

Alecksander assured himself M would declare her innocent without delay. *As I ken she be. In short time M should be on his way in search of another as evil as he.*

Miss Valerie will be declared innocent and everyone's life will resume. I need no one.

****

"He be gone."

Valerie's heart squeezed at Scotty's words. The pit of her stomach deadened. Shock beset her. "'He be gone'? How do ye ken this?" she asked.

Scotty's little face blanked into such an expression of innocence, Valerie knew she'd caught him at something.

"I worried about ye and snuck out after ye set to rest. I needed to follow that witch hunter into Smithton to be sure he did as promised," Scotty gushed in one breath.

"Promised?"

"Another witch hunter waited there for him!" Scotty continued. "Then Alecksander left town!"

The anxious little fellow fretted with the loose strings on his threadbare jacket, and confessed, "I ken not to whence he be gone."

Alecksander be gone?

"Another hath arrived?" Icy fear erased everything in Valerie's mind. "Does that make matters worse?"

Scotty gave her a slow nod. His soulful eyes bathed her in his sympathy. "I think so. This new one is supposed a much stronger and more mean witch hunter." The threads snapped between his fingers and their source.

"Do not be so anxious," Valerie comforted. "Alecksander be a famous witch hunter. 'Tis to be sure he left because he found me not to be a witch.

"This new one be sure to follow him soon." *Alecksander left me here to face this alone?*

Chapter Twenty-Nine

"But Alecksander promised me!" Scotty wailed with a stomp of his foot.

Valerie recalled her earlier wonder. "Promised ye?" She fell to her knees on the grass in front of him and placed her hands on his shoulders. "What did he promise ye?"

Scotty's lips squeezed into a thin white line, and then he spoke. "I ken ye be not a witch."

Valerie pulled him into a hug. "I ken that, dear child." She pushed back to look into his eyes again and repeated, "But I pray thee, tell me what did he promise ye?"

"We made a deal the other night."

"When we cooked thy fish?"

"Yes. We even shook on it."

Valerie remembered her observance of their 'lord and son' discussion. "Yes, I saw that. The bond ye two expressed touched my heart."

"We shook hands because he promised me he wouldn't turn ye over of witchery."

Mayhap I misheard his words. Mayhap he believed I be a witch. Mayhap 'tis wherefore he left, so he be not the one to give me to the colonists.

Scotty continued through her thoughts, "He told me he liked ye."

"I thought so, too," she softly considered. *Mayhap 'tis wherefore he left.*

"He lied to me," Scotty blurted in a fit of obvious frustration.

"No, child. Mayhap he found he didn't believe in my innocence after he told ye that." Valerie searched through every aspect of her memory, but found no reason why he wouldn't believe her innocent of witchcraft.

Did I saith something that incriminated me? "Mayhap, since ye saith he liked me, he left the hunt to this other man so he would not be the one who named me a

witch. No. He did not lie to ye
. . ." she trailed off.
They comforted each other
until late in the evening.
"I'd best be getting back to
the colonial home now," Scotty
eventually told her. "They won't
have even missed me. They'll just
think I've been hiding from them
when they see me again."
"Wherefore return to that
horrid place?" Valerie wondered to
him.
"I want to be in Smithton to
keep an ear out for the new witch
hunter's plans."
Valerie's heart lifted at his
words. *The boy be on constant
thought of my good.*
"I will think of something I
can do," he finished.
Valerie squeezed him. "Thank
ye, lad. I believe *we* will think
of something *we* can do." She
ushered him out the door with the
words, "Now hurry on with ye
before morning breaks."
Valerie watched the child go
until he disappeared into the
darkness, but envisioned
Alecksander as *he* left her. *I do
sense our connection.*
****

The muscles in Alecksander's chest tightened as he rode away from the township, but he ignored the curious sensation. After a few days on the trail; he could bear the torturous growth of apprehension no longer.

He pulled up on his horse and turned to look back into the distant horizon. A lump grew in his throat and he acknowledged what he already knew.

Valerie existed somewhere behind him. *She does sense our connection. I should never have left her there alone. This must be remedied.*

Without another thought he wheeled his mount around. *I will make things right between us.* Penumbra swiftly carried him day and night toward their destination.

As Smithton neared, many voices wailed into Alecksander's ears. It heightened his tension. He and Penumbra thundered into town on a vacant main street.

People on their knees in positions of strident prayer overflowed the distant church doors. *'Tis this? Every settler in Smithton be at church.*

Alecksander searched for Valerie, but he couldn't see her. *I must find her. Certes she is in the church.* He rode as close to the house of worship as he could and leapt from his saddle.

He left Penumbra ground-tied behind the many mournful settlers in the middle of the street. Their cries became words to his ears as he threaded his way through their prostrate bodies.

"Dear God, we pray thee, forgive us our sinful mistakes."

Mistakes? A knot formed at the base of Alecksander's throat. Pain forbade his swallow. Tears threatened him. *Valerie? Where be thee?*

Alecksander searched all the distressed faces he passed until he stood inside the church. There, one voice boomed over the rest.

One of the judges who presided over the witch trials issued a public apology for his verdicts, "I pray thee, dear God Almighty! We are but thy humble servants, imperfect. Please forgive us the error of our ways!"

The judge hushed at Alecksander's presence. All the grief-stricken faces turned toward him. The city official stared at him with malice.

"What does this mean?" Alecksander asked the first man he came into contact with.

The man melted into a panicked confession. "We have acted too rashly. M pointed out to us all those he deemed practitioners of witchcraft. On his word we punished them all with death. But there were too many! Soon we looked at our own family members!"

He raised his hands to heaven in silence, and then continued, "We have seen the error of our ways. They could not have all been witches! Now we know our mistake and pray that God in His Glorious Majesty will forgive us."

The lump in Alecksander's throat grew to a huge proportion. His chest ached. The great man trembled. "Miss Valerie?"

The man he questioned again hailed heaven for forgiveness as an answer.

Alecksander's movements ceased. He stared at the man he questioned. The witch hunter's empty eyes roved over all those with him inside the church.

The man at his side again
spoke, as if in an effort to
absolve himself of his heinous
act. "'Tis the devil himself took
us over."
Alecksander returned his
attention to the penitent soul who
blubbered beside him. *M be the
devil himself.*
"The woman you speak of pled
herself innocent, which proved her
guilt in our possessed madness."
"I ken she be innocent,"
Alecksander murmured.
"This be our day of official
humiliation," another wailed.
"Where is M?" Alecksander
could think of no other way to
make things right with Miss
Valerie. *I will find him. I
needs must destroy him.*
"He be gone," a bystander
answered.
Alecksander voiced his
thought, "I will find him." He
put his palms to his ears. *I must
leave this incessant cacophony
before I go mad, myself.* He
almost tripped over the small soul
at his side.
"Mr. Alecksander." Scotty
sobbed.
The witch hunter leaned over
and lifted the boy into his arms.

Scotty dissolved into him
with a wave of tears. "I am
afraid."
"I ken." Alecksander ached
with his own sadness at what could
have been. *I should have done
different.* A tear escaped him.
He placed the boy on the floor.
Scotty reached for the man's
hand. Hand in hand they drew on
each other's humanity and left the
church.
Penumbra nickered, ready to
carry them both away. When Scotty
pulled Alecksander away from the
horse, he remembered another time
of Scotty's insistence.
"Ye be with me now. There be
no more need for fear. Tell me,
Scotty, what be ye reason to run
this time?"
"We must go! Ye must get me
away from here! I can be here no
more."
A concerned colonist passed
and patted the boy's shoulder.
"Take him home, sir. Today's
happenings be too much for him to
bear."
Alecksander nodded to the
settler and attempted to usher
Scotty away.
"No!" the boy demanded in
resistance to their direction.

His quiet voice filled with excitement. "We cannot leave!"

Alecksander's breath thrilled through his throat. Scotty's changed demeanor gave him reason for hope. He placed both his hands on the boy's shoulders to hold his attention.

Scotty twisted from under Alecksander's control and ran off. "The boy be in hysterics," the witch hunter mentioned in an aside to the nearby colonists.

Alecksander followed, to where his keen vision soon saw an abandoned shed. It wouldn't exist to the naked eye of a colonist. Mud and bushes, grass and tree needles, hid it.

The presence of the derelict building surprised even him in its overgrown condition.

Wherefore? He saw Scotty nowhere, and called out, "Scotty?" No answer came back to him.

WHOOSH! A puff of dust appeared, out of which came Scotty. Alecksander wondered over it for an instant, until his heart leapt and clogged his throat. Tears blurred his vision.

"Valerie?" he whispered.

"Alecksander!" she squealed as she ran toward him.

"How?" he puzzled over why he hadn't known as he caught her in his arms. Now he knew the true reason his gut forced his return.

"Scotty took good care of me," she gushed. "I'm glad he's so good at hiding."

The boy pointed at Alecksander and snickered, "I even hid her from *you*!"

Penumbra nickered as they approached. Alecksander lifted Valerie onto the horse's muscled back and jumped up to be seated behind her. Scotty gripped one of Alecksander's legs and clambered up behind them.

The witch hunter sensed the little boy's oneness with him and the natural healer. Sweet herbal fragrances wafted from Valerie's hair and body.

A surge of masculine protectiveness tensed Alecksander, but he knew he couldn't remain at their sides. *I needs must find a safe place for them, until I'm able to return.*

Business with M waited.

THE END

Read more about Valerie, Alecksander, and Scotty's future and past lifetimes - and their search for family - in the remaining two books of the CONNECTIONS Series!

~~~~

Thank you for taking time to read FATED. If you enjoyed it, please consider telling your friends or posting a short review. Word of mouth is an author's best friend and much appreciated.

Made in the USA
Charleston, SC
01 May 2015